THE KID

FROM

COURAGE

BY

RON BERMAN

www.scobre.com
www.thekidfromcourage.com

Scobre Press Corporation
2255 Calle Clara
La Jolla, CA 92037

Scobre Press books may be purchased for educa-
tional, business or sales promotional use.

First Scobre edition published 2003.

"The Dream Series"

Edited by Ramey Temple
Cover Art by Larry Salk
Cover Layout by Michael Lynch

ISBN 0-9741997-2-9

www.scobre.com

To all the dreamers...

We at Scobre Press are proud to bring you another book in our "Dream Series." In case this is your first Scobre book, here's what we're all about: the goal of Scobre is to influence young people by entertaining them with books about athletes who act as role models. The moral dilemmas facing the athletes in a Scobre story run parallel to situations facing many young people today. After reading a Scobre book, our hope is that young people will be able to respond to adversity in their lives in the same heroic fashion as do the athletes depicted in our books.

This book is about Bryan Berry, the Kid from Courage. Born and raised in a small town, he wonders if his dreams of tennis stardom are farfetched and unattainable. But when he develops an unlikely friendship with an old tennis coach, he discovers that old school values haven't gone out of style.

The Kid from Courage offers an in-depth look at the world of a junior tennis player-the training, the competition, and the ups and downs of trying to succeed in one of the most challenging sports in the world.

We invite you now to come along with us, sit down, get comfortable, and read a book that will dare you to dream. Scobre dedicates this book to all the people who are chasing down their own dreams. We're sure that Bryan will inspire you to reach for the stars.

Here's Bryan..."The Kid from Courage."

For Milt

CHAPTER ONE

A FUNNY OLD MAN

"Ladies and gentlemen, the championship match is ready to begin!" Sixteen-year-old Jimmy Ellis was joking, of course. He was always kidding around. He glanced at a make-believe crowd before looking at me. "All set, Bryan?"

"Yeah, sure," I called out. I took a deep breath, trying to relax. *C'mon, Bryan, there's no reason to feel any pressure.* I wasn't expected to beat the best player at Courage High School. Still, I'd been looking forward to this practice match all week. As a four-teen-year-old freshman, I wanted to see how I compared to the number one player on the team.

Jimmy served, and our practice match was under way. My backhand return landed short, just past the service line. Jimmy quickly moved forward and

1

swung with his big lefty forehand. He hit the ball crosscourt for a winner.

Jimmy Ellis was a great athlete who played many sports. While I worked on my tennis every single day, he only played during tennis season. He just didn't love the game as much as I did. We had become friends a couple of years earlier, when we practiced together at the local club. Even though I played twice as much as he did, I still couldn't catch up to him. Today was no different. As always, Jimmy's power and skill on the tennis court were too much for me to handle. I tried as hard as I could, but he still won very easily, 6-1, 6-2.

On the final point of the match, Jimmy hit his best serve of the entire day—he crushed the ball right down the middle for an ace. We both walked up to the net and shook hands. "You were hitting the ball pretty well out there, Bryan. I'm gonna have to watch out for you." Even though Jimmy joked around a lot, he actually sounded like he meant it.

"Thanks, Jimmy, but you were just toying with me out there. Dude, you should really start working hard on your game. If you practiced more, you could be one of the best sixteen-year-olds in the country." It was true, Jimmy had so much potential. But tennis had never been a priority for him.

Jimmy grinned widely, "That's what Coach Anderson keeps saying." He reached into his tennis bag and took out a baseball cap. He carefully put it on, covering up his spiked blonde hair. Jimmy's wild, ever-changing hairstyles were famous at Courage High.

By comparison, I was neat and clean-cut. My short brown hair and white tennis clothes probably made me look a little nerdy. That didn't bother me. What *did* bother me, however, was my size. I was almost fifteen, and only five-feet-six-inches tall. Most pro tennis players are much bigger and stronger than that. My dad told me not to worry. He said he'd grown six inches right around the time he was my age. He predicted that I would end up being six-feet tall, just like him. I hoped he was right.

Jimmy started to walk off the court. I followed him, and then stopped, "Hey, you wanna keep playing?" I always wanted more tennis, especially after losing a match.

Jimmy seemed to think this was funny. "Naw, dude, I gotta leave. The guys and me are going to the football game. They're picking me up in an hour. Courage High is gonna destroy Lincoln High tonight! You can come with us if you want."

This was a tempting offer. Here it was, only the middle of November, and I had the chance to hang out with Jimmy and his friends. That was pretty cool because older kids at Courage High didn't normally mix with freshmen. Still, I turned him down in favor of some extra practice.

"Um, thanks, it sounds fun, but I need to get a little more tennis in."

"I should have guessed," Jimmy laughed. "Man, I've never seen anyone play as much tennis as you. Does it really mean that much to you?"

"Yep." I picked up my racket and waved it in the motion of my forehand. "I don't have your athletic talent, that's for sure. But I'm still gonna try to get one of the top spots on the tennis team." I joked, "The word around school is that the best player on the team has crazy hair and almost never practices."

Jimmy smiled in agreement, "That is *so* true, Bryan. Okay, I'm out, see you at school tomorrow."

"All right, Jimmy, thanks for playing."

After getting a drink from the water fountain, I sat down and thought about the match. I was very unhappy with the way I'd played. I knew that Jimmy was a more experienced player, especially with a year of high school tennis under his belt. I reminded myself that he was also older than me. None of these things made me feel any better. The bottom line was that I simply didn't get the job done out there.

On a brighter note, I felt good about having a friend as cool as Jimmy. This was important because I was pretty shy. This was my first year of high school and I was trying hard to fit in. I started to think that I should have accepted Jimmy's offer and gone to the football game with the guys. Instead, I grabbed a bucket of balls and practiced my serve.

Later that night, I lay in bed unable to sleep. The defeat I had suffered that afternoon was still in my mind. *I should have gone to the net more. My serve was awful.* Pictures of my match with Jimmy raced through my head. This wasn't unusual for me. Nothing—absolutely nothing—was more important to me than tennis.

I lived in the state of Kansas, in a small town called Courage. Nothing important ever seemed to happen there. Maybe that's why my dream of becoming a professional tennis player sometimes seemed crazy. Yes, I was ranked in my state—twenty-third in the fourteen and under division. However, I knew that this didn't mean very much. When it came to junior tennis, Kansas wasn't very well known. If I lived in a different state, like California or Florida, I wouldn't even be ranked in the top one hundred.

I sat up in my bed and leaned against the pillow, deep in thought. Tennis is one of the most competitive sports in the world. I wondered if I actually had a chance to make it. Even though I had some doubts, I was certain of one thing—*nobody* wanted it more than I did. Sure, there were skilled junior players all over the country. They were competing in national tennis tournaments and training with the best coaches in the country. As for me, I lived in the middle of nowhere—in a town so small it only had one movie theater. Still, I was determined that Bryan Berry of Courage, Kansas, would somehow find a way.

I just *had* to make it. It was fate. Five years ago, I discovered tennis by accident. I found a tennis racket and a can of used balls in a box of Dad's old stuff in our garage. After spending a few hours hitting those yellow balls against our garage door, I was hooked. Brandon, my younger brother, liked basketball and baseball, but tennis became my sport. It changed my life forever.

Tennis had always been popular in Courage. Twelve years earlier, the town had built "The Courage Courts and Recreation Club," a beautiful public tennis club. Right away, it became known to everyone simply as "The Courts." With six tennis courts, a gym, and a pool, this indoor club became very popular. I had practically *lived* there for the past three years. I went to The Courts every single day after school to play tennis. I usually stayed until I had to be home for dinner. On weekends, if I wasn't in a tournament, I could be found there all day.

In between matches, I spent most of my time in the big lounge area upstairs. That's where everyone hung out. I would watch TV, do my homework, or just listen to the adults talk. Their discussions were usually loud and entertaining. I liked it best when they argued about sports.

I laughed softly as I thought about one of the adults, a funny old man named Henry Johnson. Whenever the conversation turned to tennis, his voice was always the loudest. "Old Man" Johnson had said many times that the champions from his youth were greater than the players of today. His opinions were usually

6

met with laughter.

"Give me a break, Henry!" The men always argued, "Players today hit the ball harder than those past champions could have even dreamed!"

Johnson would usually respond by telling one of his many tennis stories. He liked to speak of the time when A. J. Bradford hit the biggest serve ever at Wimbledon. "It was so fast, nobody even *saw* the ball!" Johnson would declare with excitement in his voice. He claimed that a big cloud of dust right on the line proved that the ball was good.

Another tale focused on a doubles match that took place back in 1945. The most famous player on the court was Danny Crawford, a superstar at that time. One of the players on the other team was doing a lot of trash talking. Crawford became very annoyed. He warned his opponent to be quiet, but the talk continued. Old Man Johnson said that Crawford finally found a way to shut the guy up—he hit a return of serve so hard, it nailed his opponent square in the stomach!

Although I sort of doubted that Johnson's stories were actually true, I liked hearing them. I sometimes wondered about the old man's past. Rumor had it that he once coached a great young tennis player named Johnny Matthews. Tragically, Matthews died just when he was becoming a star. From what I'd heard, his death was so upsetting to Johnson that he never coached again.

Although Johnson was a harmless old man, it was unclear how much he really knew about tennis. People around The Courts said that he was totally out of touch, maybe even slightly crazy. I had no way of knowing if any of that stuff was true, because Johnson and I had never spoken.

Growing tired, I leaned my head back down on my pillow. I wondered why I was laying awake thinking about Henry Johnson. I certainly had more important things to worry about than a crazy old man who hung around at The Courts.

CHAPTER TWO

THE COURAGE OPEN

Two months later, I jumped out of bed early on a freezing Saturday morning in January. It was the day of the "Courage Open," a local tennis tournament. Once again, the best players in town would compete for the club championship. This was the one tournament each year that wasn't divided into age groups—it was "open," which meant that both kids and adults could play. Although I had never advanced beyond the second round, I felt good about my chances this year. I had recently celebrated my fifteenth birthday, so I knew that I was older and stronger than last year.

When I arrived at The Courts, I went straight upstairs to check in at the tournament desk. I smiled when I saw Mrs. Fletcher sitting there. She was a true tennis fan who had always shown interest in my tennis career.

"Good morning, Bryan," she said, flashing a bright smile.

"How are you, Mrs. Fletcher?" I asked politely.

"I'm always happy when the tournament comes around. How about you?"

"I'll let you know after my match."

She laughed, "I'm sure you'll do fine. Let's see, you're playing Jeff Harris in the first round." Leaning forward, she whispered with a smile, "Play his backhand, Bryan. It's his weak spot."

"Thanks for the tip, Mrs. Fletcher. I'll remember that."

Now that I had checked in, I sat down and waited for my match to be called. I took a look around. I'd been coming to The Courts for a long time and I knew the place inside out. The six tennis courts were on the first floor, in two rows of three. Also downstairs was the gym, pool, and locker rooms. A winding staircase led up to the huge lounge where I was sitting at the moment. In the corner there was a snack bar called "The Courts Grill." I had eaten hundreds of their cheeseburgers! The lounge had windows that overlooked the courts, which made it easy to watch the tennis below. All around the room there were couches and chairs so people could sit back and relax. Over on the far side of the lounge, there was a big-screen TV.

Hearing my name on the loudspeaker, I picked up my tennis bag and walked back over to the tournament desk. Mrs. Fletcher handed me a can of balls and made the introductions, "Bryan, you know Mr. Harris, don't you?"

"Yeah, sure, how's it going?" I shook his hand nervously.

During our ten-minute warm-up, I checked out my adult opponent. I smiled for a moment, realizing that Mrs. Fletcher was right about Mr. Harris's slice backhand. He seemed to get under it too much, resulting in a ball that floated lazily through the air.

As the match got under way, I started out a little slowly. A couple of mistakes cost me the opening game, but it didn't take me long to settle down. After winning the first set, 6-2, I was on a roll. By the time it was 4-1 in the second set, the match seemed like a lock. Knowing that Jimmy Ellis was playing two courts away, I looked over to see how he was doing. It seemed like he was crushing his opponent. Jimmy was the sixth "seed." Like all tournaments, the Courage Open listed the top players in order of how well they were expected to do. For a moment, I thought about how cool it would be if I were one of the top seeds—that would mean I was one of the best players in Courage.

Mr. Harris took advantage of the fact that I wasn't paying close attention. He won a couple of games very quickly. I was still leading 4-3, but I was upset with my lack of focus. I told myself to play harder. *Get your head back into the game, Bryan!*

With my mind back on my own match, I held my serve with four straight points. I went on to win the match, 6-2, 6-4. When I walked back upstairs after the match, my mother cheerfully said to me, "That was good tennis, Bryan. You looked terrific out there."

"Thanks, Mom. I didn't play my best, though. I'm gonna have to play much better when I face Mr. Kaplan." Randy Kaplan, my next opponent, had breezed through the first round earlier that morning. It was going to take a much stronger effort to get past him.

After my mom left, I decided to check out the results of some of the other matches. I walked over to the "draw." This was a large piece of cardboard that listed all the matches and scores. Jimmy Ellis was standing there. "What's up, Jimmy?"

"Hey, Bryan!" We exchanged knuckle bumps. "What was your score?"

"6-2, 6-4," I answered. "How about you?"

"Two bagels." Jimmy smiled. A bagel meant zero. Once again, Jimmy had passed through the opening round without losing a single game.

"Who do you play in the second round?" I asked.

"Second round?" Jimmy rolled his eyes. "I'm not worried about the second round. I'm trying to get ready for Kenny Singleton. He's gonna be waiting for me in the quarters. I hear he's been hitting the ball great lately."

I wished I could be as confident as Jimmy. There was no doubt in his mind that he was going to reach the quarterfinals! He carefully studied the draw, which was updated hourly by Mrs. Fletcher. "If you win your second-round match, chances are you'll play Ted Grover in the third round." Jimmy smiled at the thought of this match-up. "The all-American kid, Bryan Berry, against Ted 'The Jerk' Grover. I could sell tickets for that one! Dude, that guy is a lowdown cheater." It was true. Ted Grover was a very rude adult with a terrible reputation around The Courts. The thought of facing him wasn't very pleasant.

We continued checking out the draw, discussing likely match-ups. Then, Jimmy and I walked over to the large window that overlooked court number one. Mike Scully, the top seed in the tournament, was playing. He was putting the finishing touch on an easy first-round victory. Scully, thirty-five years old and a former pro, was the best player around.

The two of us stood with our noses stuck to the glass window, watching the action. Scully hit winners and cracked big serves that landed right on the lines. "Man, he's got skills," I remarked.

"That's no joke," Jimmy replied. "Wasn't he ranked in the top hundred in the world before he retired from pro tennis?"

"Sure was. If that knee injury hadn't cut his

career short, who knows how far he could have gone?"

It wasn't long before Scully reached match point. He hit a booming ace to close out the easy victory. Jimmy shook his head. "Well, the streak continues. Five years and counting." Jimmy was talking about Scully's amazing record at the Courage Open. He had been the champion for *five* straight years. Nobody expected this year to be any different.

A few minutes later, Mike Scully walked up to the tournament desk to report his winning score. I stared at him, wondering if I could ever reach his level in tennis. Ever since I first started coming to The Courts, I had looked up to Mike. I even modeled my game after his. He was the greatest player I had ever watched in person. I had dreamed many times about playing against him in the Courage Open. The match would take place on court number one in front of everyone. People would be shocked as I pulled off the upset.

For the time being, though, I would settle for making it past the second round. Jimmy left to get a haircut, so I looked around for something to do. The huge lounge was busy with activity. It was much more crowded than usual because of the tournament. Some people were eating breakfast, while others sat around and watched the tennis.

Over on the far side of the room, a group of men were gathered around a table. They talked as they watched the tournament action. They were having a loud discussion about tennis. I could hear Old Man Johnson's sharp, clear voice. He was yelling out to the crowd, "C'mon, fellas, give me a break. Just look at the powerful tennis rackets the pros all use today. If the players from my day could have used the same rackets—forget about it! You wanna talk about power? In 1937, Arthur Peyton was playing the US Nationals against…"

I laughed to myself—*there he goes again!* It was always fun to sit around and listen to Johnson argue with the other men. He stood up in front of them, waving his hands and talking excitedly. Watching the men argue about sports was the perfect way to pass some time until my second-round match.

A couple of hours later, I checked in with Mrs. Fletcher at the tournament desk. Then I went and looked at the draw. A quick glance showed that the top eight seeds had all advanced without losing a single set. The tournament had a field of sixty-four players, so there were two rounds today and two more rounds tomorrow. The semifinals and finals would be played next weekend. I hoped that I would be playing in one of those matches.

My next opponent, Randy Kaplan, was a serve-and-volley player who attacked the net at every opportunity. When the match began, I held serve. Then I hit a couple of great backhand passing shots to gain an early break of serve. My two-handed topspin back-hand was my big weapon. It was a stroke that had always come naturally to me. By comparison, my fore-hand was a flat stroke that wasn't nearly as good. My serve wasn't that great, either. This was troubling because I knew that tennis players are supposed to be good with all of their strokes.

Playing well, I took the first set, 6-3. Then, with-out warning, my serve broke down and my whole game fell apart. Kaplan started chipping my weak second serve and coming to the net. This strategy helped him win the second set, 6-1. Suddenly, everything was going wrong for me. The momentum clearly favored Kaplan as he moved out to a four-games-to-three lead in the third set.

At 4-3, 30-all, Kaplan took a big cut at his first serve but missed long. After adjusting the strings on his racket, he tossed the ball up and swung at his sec-ond serve. The ball caught the top of the net and fell back to his side. A huge double fault! Kaplan's error set up a break point for me. He stood still for an instant, as though he couldn't believe what had just happened. His worried look gave me an extra boost of confidence.

Now serving at 30-40, Kaplan tried to attack the net. I was ready for it, belting a dipping topspin return with my two-handed backhand. Kaplan tried to make a very difficult volley. Once again, the ball caught the top of the net and rolled back to his side.

Kaplan seemed very upset. Sure, the match was still dead even—4-all in the third set. However, it appeared as though he couldn't stop thinking about those two important points. A better player would have just forgotten about it and continued to fight. Instead, the match slipped away from Kaplan. I won it, 7-5 in the third set.

I accepted congratu'itions from Mom and Dad, and Brandon too. But I realized that I had been lucky to win the match. I was disappointed and began to question myself: *I'm fifteen years old, a tournament player—how am I still struggling with ordinary players like Randy Kaplan? Have I stopped improving? Is this as good as I'm going to get?*

I wasn't too happy with myself, but I tried to remain positive. I had won both of my matches. It felt good to reach the third round, although I knew that things were about to get much tougher. As Jimmy had correctly predicted, my next opponent was Ted Grover. I was going to have to battle the biggest jerk in Courage!

I was so tired that I didn't even stop to look at the draw. Scores of other matches didn't really matter to me at that moment. I went straight home with my family and spent the evening relaxing. I tried hard to forget about Ted Grover. As soon as my head hit the pillow at ten-thirty, I was fast asleep.

CHAPTER THREE

AFRAID TO LOSE

The next morning, I arrived at The Courts and went straight upstairs to check in. My heart started to beat a little faster when I saw Ted Grover staring me down. *C'mon Bryan, he's just trying to intimidate you. Don't let him get to you.* But it was difficult not to feel worried. Grover's skills alone would make him a tough guy to beat. To make matters worse, he had a big-time reputation for "hooking," or cheating.

The first few games showed just how much pressure Grover and I were feeling. We were both "pushing," which means carefully keeping the ball in play. It was understandable why we were so nervous. Reaching the quarterfinals of the Courage Open would be a major accomplishment. This was something both of us *really* wanted.

By the time the first set reached 6-all and went to a tiebreaker, the pressure was intense. People had crowded around the large window upstairs. I saw my mom, dad, and Brandon, rooting for me. I also noticed Jimmy Ellis and some of my friends. To my surprise, even Old Man Johnson was watching.

Much to my delight, I opened up the tiebreaker by serving an ace. It gave me confidence, and I started playing some sharp tennis. After I won a couple of quick points, Grover suddenly seemed unsure of himself. He made some mistakes that helped me win the tiebreaker, 7-3. The first player to win seven points in a tiebreaker is awarded the set, but only if he's up by at least two points. Otherwise the players keep playing until someone moves ahead by two points. I won the tiebreaker, which counted as one game—which meant that I won the first set by a score of 7-6.

Way to go, Bryan! I felt good about coming through in the tiebreaker. I wondered if my opponent would get discouraged and give up without a fight. Unfortunately, Ted Grover started coming back. He played a very solid second set, breaking my serve at 4-all to grab the lead. I was mad at myself. *A double fault, a lousy forehand, it's like I'm just giving the set away.*

At 5-4, 30-all, Grover chipped a ball to the corner and rushed to the net. Sliding to my left, I smacked my two-handed backhand. I hit the ball perfectly, just beyond his reach. The ball landed on the line. I pumped my fist in excitement.

"Out!" Grover exclaimed loudly.

What? I stared at my opponent in shock. "Mr. Grover, that ball was right on the line."

"No, it was a little wide," Grover said.

There wasn't much I could do. I looked up to see who was watching from upstairs. Jimmy Ellis motioned with his hands that the ball had been good. I was angry, but I needed to keep my concentration because Grover now had a set point. After he missed his first serve, I jumped all over his second serve to fight my way back to deuce.

We continued to battle for this important game. Eventually, Grover found himself with another set point. After a brief rally, he charged to the net behind a deep approach shot. I hit a sweet topspin lob that totally fooled him. The ball landed on the baseline. Grover didn't even chase after it. Instead, he simply pointed "out" with one finger and walked over to the sideline. I rushed over and said, "Not again, Mr. Grover! C'mon, you know that one was good!"

"It was definitely close. Barely missed, as a matter of fact." Grover held out his fingers to indicate an inch. "Tied up, one set all."

"That—that's just an outright hook!" I yelled. I was steaming mad.

Mr. Grover glared at me, which suddenly made me a little nervous. He was a scary-looking man with a bald head and an ugly scar running down the side of his face. I didn't want to continue this conversation, so I decided to forget what had just happened. We were about to play a deciding third set and I needed to keep my focus.

By the time it got to 3-all in the third, the pressure was *really* on. Unfortunately, I wasn't handling it too well, and I started pushing. Grover attacked my serve and came to the net. I tossed up a short lob, which he smashed for a winner. Then, on the next point, I missed a forehand by a mile. Finally, at 15-40, I nervously hit a double fault into the bottom of the net. This put Grover in the lead, 4-3. As we switched sides he stared right at me and barked, "No punk kid is gonna stop me from getting to the quarters." I quickly looked away, because I knew that he was just trying to intimidate me.

I was determined to come back and win the match. I forced myself to keep fighting, but I simply couldn't get my game back on track. Just fifteen minutes later, it was match point. Grover hit a ball to my forehand, which I missed into the net. He immediately raised his fist, happily yelling, "YEAH!" I grabbed my stuff and slowly walked up the stairs. I was pretty upset. My parents greeted me with words of wisdom. "You gave him a heck of a run, Bryan." Dad patted me on the back.

Jimmy Ellis shook his head. "You were robbed, dude. He hooked you."

Although many people told me that I'd played a fine match, I felt totally discouraged. I just wanted to be alone. After changing my shirt in the locker room, I wandered into the gym. Nobody was in there, so I sat down on one of the benches at the far end. I tried to figure out what had gone wrong in my match.

Lost in thought, I suddenly heard the sound of approaching footsteps. I quickly looked up. To my surprise, Old Man Johnson was standing just a few feet in front of me. *What does he want?* I ignored him and stared down at the ground. This didn't seem to bother him one bit. He took a seat next to me.

"When the match is on the line, that's not the time to play scared," Johnson declared. "3-all in the third set is when you need to step it up."

"Yeah, but I…I was nervous. I didn't want to start missing shots and lose the match."

"It's okay. You're not the only junior player who has ever had trouble dealing with the pressure of a big match. Let me tell you what I used to say to juniors back in the old days. Maybe it'll help you the next time you're in that type of situation."

Something about the tone of Johnson's voice grabbed me. Or maybe it was the intensity in his eyes, or the expression on his face. Suddenly I was paying strict attention. "Bryan, every junior has to learn how to fight through nerves. That's why these are such important words." He paused, and then said, "If you're afraid to lose, you can't win."

With this comment still hanging in the air, Johnson stood up and walked away.

Three days later I was back at The Courts, warming up for a practice match with a kid named Dwight Armstrong. *If you're afraid to lose, you can't win.* It felt like those words were flashing in my head over and over again. Just as the match was getting under way, I noticed something interesting. Old Man Johnson was watching from the window upstairs. I threw the ball high into the air and swung mightily. Boom! A blazing ace right down the center of the court. I looked up again to see if Mr. Johnson was still there. Yep. Suddenly I was playing inspired tennis, hitting the ball sharply and with confidence.

This was my best day of tennis in a long time. I turned out an impressive, 6-2, 6-1, victory. As soon as it was over, I ran upstairs and approached Johnson.

"Is that what you meant by not being afraid to lose?" I asked.

"Sure was," Mr. Johnson answered. Smiling, he added, "Too bad the Courage Open wasn't today. That's how you should have played against Grover."

I chuckled, "Yeah, you're right. Of course, Grover did steal the second set with a couple of terrible calls."

"What? Ted Grover was *cheating*?" Mr. Johnson's make-believe surprise made me laugh out loud. "I know what he did, Bryan. I saw it with my own two eyes. However, the fact remains that your game broke down in that third set. It's too bad, because you did some good things in the match—especially in the first-set tiebreaker."

"Yeah, I was on a roll," I said. I tried to sound cheerful as I continued, "Oh well, at least I have something to build on. I have to start somewhere."

"Yes, you do. But you're going about it all wrong."

"What do you mean?" I leaned in closer.

"Well, you obviously work hard, but that's not enough." Johnson took off his old-fashioned eyeglasses. "The only thing that matters is that you develop proper form and technique. You're gonna have to start from scratch with some of your strokes. That's the only way you'll be able to take your game to the next level."

"From scratch?" I contemplated this thought. "But won't I start losing all the time?"

"You might—at first." He looked right at me. "All you juniors are too focused on trying to win. You forget that you're still learning the game. You have to develop your strokes and overcome your weaknesses. But it's impossible if all you care about is winning. Trust me, kid, if you don't fix the flaws in your game, they'll come back to hurt you one day."

This statement was alarming, but it also made a lot of sense. I'd always known that my serve and forehand were lousy and needed a ton of work.

"Bryan," Johnson continued, "I've been around

this game forever. That's long enough to recognize a kid whose game isn't developing properly. Your match with Grover proved it to me. These problems aren't gonna go away on their own."

I must have looked a little sad, because he patted me on the shoulder. "On the bright side, you have potential. The way you move around out there is very natural. You can't teach that stuff." He leaned back in his chair. "Watching you play reminds me of someone I used to coach a long time ago." He stared at the wall behind me for a few seconds. I asked, "Does it mean anything that I'm ranked twenty-third in Kansas in the fourteen and under division?"

Mr. Johnson smiled. "Sure it does, kid, but I'd be saying the same thing even if you were number one. There are talented juniors all over America who are working on their game every single day. It's them you want to compete with, not just the kids in Kansas. Isn't that right?"

Everything that came out of the old man's mouth made perfect sense to me. I began to wonder why everyone thought he'd lost it. "Yes, Mr. Johnson, you're right," I sighed. "I know I need help. What would it take to get my game on track?"

"Sacrifice, commitment, lots of hard work. And that's just for starters." He rose out of his chair. He was short and slim—about five-foot-seven, 130 pounds. His silver hair was thinning and combed over to one side. He had a pair of bushy eyebrows that jumped around his forehead every time he spoke. Examining his wrinkled face, I figured that he was about seventy-five years old.

"Well, I've got to be going. Promised my wife I'd be home by five today. But if you ever want to get out on the tennis court with me and do some work, let me know." He turned to leave.

"Wait a minute." I hesitated for a split second. "How about tomorrow?"

Mr. Johnson looked surprised that I was taking him up on his offer. "Tomorrow?" He paused. "Tomorrow will be fine. I'll meet you here at three thirty." With that, the old man was gone.

I wondered if asking Henry Johnson for help was crazy. *Everyone at the club thinks he's totally out of it.* It wasn't hard to understand why: his glasses looked like they were borrowed from Benjamin Franklin, his tennis racket looked like it came straight out of a museum, and all he talked about was "the old days." It didn't add up to a promising situation.

Still, I had to admit that something about Old Man Johnson interested me. I wondered, *could he possibly help me become a better tennis player?* It was a long shot, a real long shot.

CHAPTER FOUR

COACH

The next day seemed to last forever. When school finally ended, I raced home and changed into my tennis clothes. I arrived at The Courts and found Johnson upstairs reading the newspaper. It was quiet, which was normal for this hour of the day.

"How's it going, Mr. Johnson?"

"Fine, kid. Have a seat."

Johnson put down the newspaper and sat back in his chair. He was wearing a brown warm-up suit and a floppy white hat. A huge basket filled with tennis balls was on the floor next to him. His old tennis racket was resting on top of the basket.

"Bryan, every kid dreams of going pro someday, but what are your goals in tennis over the next couple of years?"

I thought about it for a second before answering, "I want to get good enough to be invited to play in national tournaments. I've always dreamed of going to Kalamazoo and competing in the National Championships." Kalamazoo was a beautiful city in the state of Michigan. It was also the place where they held the most important tournament in junior tennis.

"That's a fine goal. But let me tell you something, kid. It's a long, long way from Courage to Kalamazoo." I nodded. In terms of actual distance, Kalamazoo wasn't much more than five hundred miles from Courage. Johnson was right, though. At the moment, it was a world away for me—I would have to improve a great deal to have a chance to play there.

"Okay," he continued, "so let's get down to business and hopefully get you started on the road to Kalamazoo. Bryan, your backhand is perfect, but both your serve and forehand are very weak."

"I know," I said glumly. "That's usually the reason I lose matches."

"Well, so you need to get those strokes up to the same level as your backhand. How can you do this? You're gonna have to develop solid, dependable strokes. Then you need to hit about a million tennis balls over the next couple of years. If you do that, you'll have a chance. Let's get started, because it's gonna take a lot of hard work."

I soon found out that he wasn't kidding about

hard work. When we got out on the tennis court, Mr. Johnson stood at the net with the large basket of balls. He hit balls to my forehand, one after another. He explained how to get under the ball and loop it across the net to create topspin. This was a major change for me, and things didn't go too well. I was totally discouraged. I seemed to be getting worse and worse as we went along. When we were done, I was covered in sweat.

"That was terrible! I couldn't even keep the ball in the court."

"Doesn't matter, Bryan. It was a good start. Let's say that you hit about twenty percent of the balls correctly. Next time, you'll try to increase that number to thirty percent. The goal is to be close to one hundred percent. *That's* when you'll be the type of player who has a shot to get to Kalamazoo. You're not gonna do it all in one day."

That night I had trouble sleeping. I couldn't stop thinking about the interesting events of the afternoon. We had arranged to meet again the next day, and I found myself looking forward to it.

Mr. Johnson and I continued to practice together. A week later I found myself matched up once again with Jimmy Ellis at The Courts. I played some excellent tennis, but I also made a ton of mistakes. As usual, Jimmy destroyed me. Although Mr. Johnson had taught me some good stuff, I just couldn't seem to put all the pieces together.

The last game of the match was a perfect example. First, I played three solid points to put Jimmy in a hole, love-40. Then, just as quickly, I lost three points in a row. Soon Jimmy arrived at match point. He hit a serve out wide, pulling me off the court. I managed to stick out my racket and punch the ball back, setting off a baseline rally.

Like many other points in the match, this was an opportunity to use the lessons Mr. Johnson had taught me. I hit a topspin forehand deep in the court. I followed up that shot with a stinging backhand. Jimmy was forced out of position. He could only respond with a weak backhand that floated lazily through the air. That ball was just begging to be smacked for an easy winner! But I got confused and accidentally used my old forehand stroke. Instead of bashing a clean topspin forehand, I hit it off the frame of my racket. The result was a shot that landed very short on Jimmy's side. The talented lefty did the rest. With the greatest of ease, he belted the ball out of my reach. The point was over, and so was the match.

After Jimmy and I picked up the used tennis balls, we walked upstairs to the lounge. We bought a couple of smoothies and sat down at a table. I told Jimmy that I had been practicing with Mr. Johnson recently.

"I know, dude. Word travels fast around here." Jimmy laughed and said, "My only question is, are you *crazy*?" Jimmy jokingly made his point by lightly tapping my head with his knuckles. How could I convince him that it wasn't crazy to practice with Mr. Johnson? I couldn't even convince myself!

A little while later, after Jimmy left, I went to look for Mr. Johnson. Walking into the gym, I found the old man trying to turn on a treadmill. "I'll tell you, Bryan, I don't believe in all this stuff. In my day we didn't have any of these machines. Still, the best players could play five sets in hundred-degree heat. So what's the point of it all?"

Smiling, I replied, "Well, it's great for strength and conditioning. All you have to do is look at how good tennis players are these days. I mean, c'mon, let's be serious. You don't *really* think those players from the old days could hang today, do you?"

"I most certainly do!" Mr. Johnson exclaimed. His booming voice made me laugh. I liked hanging out with him. It was fun messing around and arguing about stuff like sports. I could honestly say that the old man and I were becoming friends. He gave me hope that I could actually make it in tennis. Nobody had ever made me feel like that before. Suddenly, without thinking, I asked, "Will you be my coach?"

Mr. Johnson stared at me for a long time before saying, "Are you sure that's what you want? A lot of people would say that you're making a mistake."

He was right. I was a pretty decent player, not to mention a ranked junior. Asking Henry Johnson to become my coach was a huge risk. Sure, the old man had been a coach in his younger days, but he hadn't accomplished much. As a matter of fact, he only had one claim to fame: he had once coached Johnny Matthews, the great junior who died. But that was over fifty years ago!

None of that stuff mattered to me. Neither did the fact that everyone seemed to view Mr. Johnson with doubt. I had big dreams, and I definitely needed some help. I was beginning to think that this strange old guy might be the right man for the job. He had coached Johnny Matthews almost to the point of becoming a star. Could he do the same thing for me?

"Are you with me, kid?"

"Yes, sir." Our eyes met and I said, "I want to become a great tennis player. There's nothing in the world I want more. Can you help me?"

As if deep in thought, Mr. Johnson looked past me and onto the tennis courts. A few seconds later, he extended his hand and I shook it. "I think I can, Bryan. Be here tomorrow at three thirty and we'll get started. We've got a lot of work to do."

The next day I showed up at The Courts with a smile on my face. I had a new coach! By the time I dragged myself home that evening, I wasn't smiling anymore. I was exhausted! I guess I hadn't been pre-pared for three long hours of running, hitting, and exercising. This was only the beginning. Mr. Johnson started training me four and five times a week. Each practice was very challenging.

During moments of rest, Mr. Johnson and I talked about tennis strategy. "Let me ask you a question, kid. You get a short ball and you attack the net. How do you decide whether you should protect the line—or instead, cover for a crosscourt shot?"

"I'd use my gut feeling."

"Yes, I agree. But there's more to it than just that. Let's say the guy is going crosscourt almost every time. On a big point, what's the smart thing to do?"

"Cover the crosscourt."

"Very good, Bryan. Yeah, maybe he hits it the other way and wins the point. But more often than not, a guy will go with his best shot. That's especially true if it's an important situation."

Each practice with my coach brought something new. We would work on tennis in ways that I had never done before. Mr. Johnson always spent the first couple of hours working on my forehand and serve. These were the two shots he was totally changing. Then we would choose one or two different strokes and hit them over and over again. Whether it was the drop shot, the drop volley, the approach shot— or anything else—we were sure to practice it.

At the end of every training session, Mr. Johnson had me do several conditioning drills. The toughest one was a "game" that forced me to run from one corner to the other until I could barely stand up anymore. I always tried to give one hundred percent no matter how tired I felt. Then we would walk into the gym, where my training would continue. Mr. Johnson favored an "old-school" program of jumping rope, push-ups, sit-ups, and jumping jacks.

These long workouts left me more exhausted than I had ever imagined possible. I didn't complain, because it was exciting to train at such a high level. It was encouraging that Mr. Johnson was by my side every step of the way, rooting me on. He was just as enthusiastic as I was. His love for the sport of tennis was awesome.

Even though I was thrilled that Mr. Johnson was my new coach, there *was* a downside. Some of the adults at The Courts thought I was making a serious mistake. They sure let me know it! To them, Henry Johnson was a crazy old man. They kept telling me that I would be better off with a younger coach.

It would have been nice to prove the adults wrong by winning some tennis matches. Unfortunately, the exact opposite was happening. I was getting killed in junior tournaments, especially because I was now in the sixteen and under division. I *still* couldn't win a set against Jimmy Ellis. I also suffered some losses to people I was used to beating.

I understood why I was having problems in my matches. For one thing, my new serve wasn't dependable yet. As a result, I was hitting a lot of double faults. But that was nothing compared to my forehand. Learning a brand-new stroke was very difficult. During matches, there were times when I would get confused. Wild shots would shoot off my racket when I used my old forehand. It was actually pretty embarrassing.

So this was a rough time for me. I expressed my frustration to Mr. Johnson, who was extremely comforting. He looked at me and said, "Bryan, you know the saying 'no pain, no gain,' right?"

"Sure," I replied.

"Well, this is an example of it. We're trying to make your game better in the long run. But you have to be willing to lose some matches in order to make that happen. I know it's frustrating, but it's the only way. I believe that it takes at least six months to build a new stroke. During that time, it's going to be rough. There will be days when you can't seem to hit the ball over the net."

"You can say that again."

Mr. Johnson laughed. "Yeah, I know, you've had some ugly matches. But you *will* be rewarded for all this pain and suffering. Trust me, kid, it'll happen for you. Once those new strokes are perfect, you'll be a totally different player."

"But I guess there's still a long road ahead of us."

"I'm afraid so, kid. These things don't happen overnight. But when everything finally falls into place, it'll be the greatest feeling in the world."

CHAPTER FIVE

JOHNNY MATTHEWS

One Saturday in April, Mr. Johnson and his wife, Elizabeth, invited me over for dinner. Mr. Johnson said that he had told her a lot about me, so I was looking forward to meeting her. After a long practice, Mr. Johnson and I left The Courts together. I trailed his old car on my bike.

The Johnson's lived in a small, one-story house on a quiet street. The outside of the house needed a paint job, but the inside was warm and inviting. Mr. Johnson introduced me to his wife. She was wearing a colorful dress, with an apron tied around her waist. She reminded me of my grandmother.

"You boys can relax in the living room until dinner is ready. Are you hungry, Bryan?"

Mr. Johnson laughed, answering for me, "I worked the kid hard today, Elizabeth. Trust me, he's hungry!" I smiled, because he was absolutely right.

"Good," said Mrs. Johnson, "I'm glad I made a lot of food. Now go sit down."

I took a seat in an old leather armchair, settling back comfortably. I noticed some framed photographs arranged neatly on the table beside me. One was of Mr. and Mrs. Johnson with the inscription:

Chicago, 1973

There was another photo that caught my eye. It showed a young Mr. Johnson with two other men in tennis clothes. "Who are these two?"

"That's me with A. J. Bradford and Danny Crawford in California, back in 1944."

I was surprised. "Wow, you really did know famous pros."

"Sure, I knew them all. I was teaching at the Los Angeles Tennis Club back then. That was the best club in the country at the time. That's where most of the top pros worked out when they were in town."

I touched the picture with my finger, "That must have been so cool."

"It sure was, those were good times. I had the best job in the world." He smiled and said, "I spent most of my time working with juniors just like you."

"Mr. Johnson," I said slowly, hesitating for a second. I was ready to ask the question I had wanted to ask for weeks now. "I—I've heard that you had a big-time junior who died." Mr. Johnson was silent for a moment. I was immediately worried that it had been a mistake to bring it up. I started to say, "I'm sorry, forget that I even—"

"It's okay, Bryan. That's true. His name was Johnny Matthews. He was a kid like you, but not as lucky. Johnny didn't even have a real home. His father was alive, but he was a no-good drunk. He wasn't even interested in taking care of his own son. When Johnny was thirteen, he started hanging around the Los Angeles Tennis Club. Sometimes he would even sneak in when the club was closed. He used to hit balls against the wall, for hours at a time. Once I caught him sleeping in the members lounge after hours. His dad had locked him out of his own house."

"When did you start training him?" I asked.

"Soon after that, when I saw how serious he was about tennis. He had never taken a lesson in his life, but he had a natural game. He moved around the court with less effort than anyone I've ever seen."

The old man paused as he got up and reached for two cans of soda. He handed one of them to me and continued, "I worked with Johnny for over four years, between 1945 and 1949. He was destroying every junior tennis player in California. I would have him work out with the pros when they were in town. Bryan, he could hang with all of them. And he was only seventeen! All he needed was a couple more years of tournament experience. I had him scheduled to play a whole summer of nationals when it happened." There was another pause as Mr. Johnson took a sip of his drink.

"What happened?" I leaned in closer.

"It was a Sunday in early June, back in '49. We had practiced in the morning as usual. I was preparing Johnny for a tournament in Santa Barbara. It was scheduled to start the next day. That night he drove out there with his doubles partner, Mark Thompson. They were the top-ranked doubles team in California. Johnny was also seeded number one in the singles draw."

Mr. Johnson paused again. I could tell he was coming to the bad part of the story. "Mark called me up late that night. He was sobbing so hard I could barely understand him. He told me that he and Johnny had stopped at a roadside restaurant to have dinner. While they were eating, two men came in carrying guns, demanding money. They also decided to kidnap the waitress. She screamed in horror, afraid of what might happen. When the men turned toward the exit, Johnny jumped up...he jumped up so quick that nobody even moved. Johnny lunged at the men, and he decked one of them. But when he turned to the other one, there was a struggle. The gun went off and Johnny got shot. He died instantly."

Mr. Johnson's voice dropped. "The papers said that he was a hero. They wrote about how he was willing to sacrifice himself to save that waitress." I could see that the old man's eyes were moist.

"The newspapers were right," I said softly. "Johnny was definitely a hero. I'm really sorry I brought back all those memories, Mr. Johnson."

"Don't be sorry. I'm glad you did. You know, I haven't told that story for almost thirty years. I've tried to forget, but I never could. It feels good to talk about Johnny again."

"Do you have a picture of him?" I asked.

"I sure do. I'll show you after dinner, okay? I'll bet you're ready to eat." He perked up and called out, "How's dinner coming, Elizabeth? You've got a hungry young tennis player in here."

Mrs. Johnson responded from the kitchen, "Perfect timing, boys. Everything is ready."

Dinner was delicious and fun. As we ate, Mr. Johnson entertained us with stories of his youth. He talked about playing tennis, serving in the army, and meeting his wife. I asked Mrs. Johnson how long they had been married. "Fifty-five years this July," she replied proudly.

"That's amazing," I said. "Fifty-five years! Do you have a secret?"

Mrs. Johnson smiled, "As a matter of fact, I do. I never remind this old man how many times he's told me his stories. I pretend they're brand-new every time I hear them!"

I laughed, "I'll remember that, Mrs. Johnson." I looked at Mr. Johnson. "People at The Courts don't seem to believe many of your stories."

He looked amused. "Yes, I know, but that doesn't bother me one bit. My life has been too good to worry about stuff like that. I've served my country, I've known legendary tennis players. And most importantly—" he looked at his wife and smiled—"I was lucky enough to marry the prettiest girl in town. So those people can say whatever they want. I really don't care." He took one last bite and smiled, "Well, I'm stuffed."

"Me too. That was an incredible dinner, Mrs. Johnson. Thank you so much."

Mrs. Johnson was very pleased, and she refused to let me help with the dishes. I got up from the table, following Mr. Johnson into a large room. It was cluttered with books and magazines. I stared at the shelves, which were overflowing with trophies. There were more than I could count. I read the inscriptions:

Winner, 1948 Los Angeles Griffith Park Boys 16 & Under, Johnny Matthews

Winner, 1949 Santa Monica Boys 18 & Under, Johnny Matthews

I continued to study the trophies one by one. Meanwhile, Mr. Johnson was seated at his big desk, shuffling through stacks of papers. He handed me a newspaper clipping that was yellow and faded. On the top Mr. Johnson had written, *"Los Angeles Times, September 19, 1948."* The headline read, "The Life and Times of Johnny Matthews." The story was printed as follows:

He came from a broken home. He used to cut classes on a regular basis. He appeared in Juvenile Court twice before his thirteenth birthday. Yet, just last week, sixteen-year-old tennis sensation Johnny Matthews capped off a summer to remember. After easily marching through the Southern California Sectionals, he remained undefeated *all* summer. It's no wonder that people have been talking about him. The word is that he just might be the future of American tennis.

Matthews uses his six-feet-two-inch frame to hit a huge cannonball serve. Together with smooth and powerful groundstrokes, it's the total package. And don't let his friendly personality fool you—this kid is as tough as nails on the court. He crushes opponents as regularly as the sun shines in California. I asked Johnny how he overcame his rocky childhood and developed such a marvelous game. His response was immediate. He said, "Three words—Coach Henry Johnson. He took me in, and gave me something better to do than get in trouble. It was difficult at first, but now it's all starting to pay off."

After speaking with Johnny, I caught up with his coach, Henry Johnson. He's one of the most well known tennis coaches in California. I asked Johnson how far Johnny Matthews could go in tennis. "The sky's the limit," he told me. "This kid is the real thing."

After reading the rest of the article, I looked over at Mr. Johnson. All of a sudden, I felt truly sorry for him. This old man deserved better luck from the sport of tennis. Without a word, he handed me a photo of himself and Johnny. They were standing in front of a tennis club, smiling and holding tennis rackets. A large sign in the background read, "Los Angeles Tennis Club." Johnny appeared to be around sixteen or seventeen years old. He was tall and thin, with messy hair and a sparkle in his eyes. He looked like a happy and confident kid.

We sat on the couch looking through more photographs and newspaper clippings about Johnny. I was starting to understand what an impact he had made on Mr. Johnson's life. That awful tragedy had changed everything. It was hard to imagine what they might have accomplished in tennis together. It made me wonder if I could ever reach Johnny's level. I looked over at the old man and asked, "Mr. Johnson, remember what you once said? That I remind you of Johnny? Did you mean as a tennis player?"

"You bet I did. You move around the court the way Johnny used to—so naturally, without effort. And you treat the game with respect and dedication, just like he did. Johnny really loved tennis, same as you."

"But my game has so many flaws."

"That may be true, Bryan, but we're going to fix them. Everything will happen in its own time." Mr. Johnson paused, chuckling softly. "It's funny, Bryan. Johnny used to worry about his game too. I'll tell you the same thing I told him: Just put the doubts out of your mind. I know you're concerned because you're losing to a few people. Believe me, it doesn't matter one bit. All you're doing is taking one step backward in order to take two steps forward. It'll be worth it, I promise."

A few minutes later I was hopping onto my bicycle in Mr. Johnson's front yard. "Thanks for everything, Mr. Johnson, I had a great time today. There's no way for me to tell you how much I appreciate all your help."

"That's nice of you to say, kid." The old man's voice was gruff, but the emotion could not be masked, "By the way, from now on, no more 'Mr. Johnson.'

Just call me Henry."

"Yes sir, uh, Henry. Thanks a lot." Then, smiling, I asked, "Did you let all your students call you Henry?"

"No," replied the old man. "Only Johnny."

I smiled as I pedaled down his winding driveway toward home.

CHAPTER SIX

SUMMER VACATION

Two months later—six months after my training with Henry had begun—I was happy that summer vacation had begun. The only bad thing was that I had suffered an ankle sprain during a match. The injury wasn't serious, but it kept me out of competition for a couple of weeks. It was a major disappointment, because it forced me to miss the "Missouri Valley Supers Circuit" tournaments. Playing in these important tournaments was the only way to get chosen for the nationals, my ultimate goal. The nationals were also tournaments, but with one big difference—only the best junior players in the whole country were allowed to play. By missing the Missouri Valley Supers Circuit tournaments, I was out of luck. I would have to wait until next year to have a chance to reach the nationals.

My disappointment didn't last long. Getting injured had been bad luck, but I was soon back to one hundred percent. I had a busy summer ahead of me. Although I couldn't play the nationals, there were plenty of other tournaments in Kansas. More importantly, with Henry pointing the way, I was making big improvements on the tennis court. As he had predicted, I was becoming a new player.

I was finally starting to hit my forehand the right way. My flat, uneven forehand had disappeared, replaced by a beautiful topspin stroke. All of a sudden, I could hit the ball anywhere I pleased. Sometimes it was hard to believe that it was me—Bryan Berry—hitting these powerful shots. It made me want to improve even more.

The many hours we had worked on the serve were beginning to pay off. Henry had changed my motion, and now it was nice and smooth. I was getting closer to the kind of serve I had always dreamed about.

As the summer raced on, I continued to train with Henry and play in tournaments. Obviously, the level of competition wasn't even close to national tournaments. Still, I was pleased that I was easily getting to the semis and finals of these events.

My success wasn't all that surprising. I had a new forehand and a dangerous new serve. My well-rounded game had put me at a new level. I was now destroying kids who had beaten me just a year earlier. Suddenly, I was known as one of the best juniors in Kansas. This honor gave me a ton of confidence.

The funny thing was that playing tournaments was the easy part. Henry's training sessions were much more difficult. He'd been taking it easy on me while I was coming back from the injury. Now that I was completely healthy, our workouts were tougher than ever.

One of the highlights of my summer came in early August. Henry and I drove for an hour and a half to watch an exhibition tennis match in the city of Wichita, Kansas. The competitors were Chris Conrad and Jake Sanders, the top two Americans in the world. I had never seen live professional tennis. The opportunity to see them play in person was overwhelming. Henry laughed loudly when I asked him if his beat-up old car was going to make it there in time.

When we arrived at the Wichita Sports Arena, excitement was definitely in the air. When Chris Conrad and Jake Sanders stepped on the court to warm up, I was the happiest kid in the whole place. As we watched the match, Henry quietly gave me tips about several things. He told me to watch a few points focusing on footwork only. He also talked about the type of strategy the players might be using in different situations.

One point was especially amazing. We watched as Jake Sanders hit a blazing serve right up the middle. The return exploded off Conrad's racket and landed deep in the court. Moving to his left, Sanders crunched a crosscourt backhand. I was sure it would be a winner, but speedy Chris Conrad was able to reach the ball. He crushed his huge topspin forehand right up the line for a winner! The crowd exploded with applause. I found myself jumping to my feet and cheering. Henry grinned at me when I sat down.

"Good tennis, huh?"

"For sure!" I couldn't believe what I was seeing. I looked at Henry and whispered excitedly, "Remember when you talked about developing solid, dependable strokes? *This* is what you meant."

"Yep. We're watching live proof of what it takes to be great. You know why these guys hit the ball so well? It isn't magic. It's perfect technique, which is the result of a lot of hard work."

Watching Chris Conrad and Jake Sanders perform with such skill was very inspiring. The next day I was back on the court, wondering if I could ever play like they did. I had three weeks left in summer until the start of school. I would be spending the last two in Los Angeles with my family. My aunt lived out there and the trip had been planned for awhile now. I was a little worried about slacking off, but Henry had a different opinion. He felt that a few weeks off would actually be good for my tennis. He didn't want me to burn out. So I set my mind to having the best week of practice ever. Henry and I spent that entire week training from dawn until dusk. By Friday afternoon I was ready for my California vacation.

Los Angeles was a lot of fun. The weather was incredible, and there was plenty to do. Both Brandon and I had a blast at Disneyland and at an awesome water park. Our whole family also did a lot of sightseeing. I even got to visit the Los Angeles Tennis Club, where Henry used to work. It was a fantastic trip.

Three days after returning from California, I was walking down the hall at Courage High. It was the first day of the new school year. Jimmy Ellis snuck up behind me and punched my shoulder. "Look, it's that movie star from Los Angeles!" He joked, "Can I have your autograph?" I laughed, rubbing my shoulder.

"I wish you could have been there, Jimmy. That city is so cool. It's totally different from Courage."

"I can imagine. Dude, you know I've never even been outside of Kansas? Here you are, Mr. Hollywood. So how was the beach?"

"It was awesome—huge waves and hot girls everywhere!"

Jimmy smiled, "Sounds like the place for a stud like me."

"Yeah *right*," I laughed. The first period bell rang and we bumped knuckles, making plans to play tennis over the weekend. A few minutes later, sitting in class, I shook my head. *Boy, did the summer go quickly!* It had started with the disappointment of the ankle injury, which kept me out of action for a couple of weeks. Happily, I quickly moved past it and ended up having an awesome summer. I was ready for the school year, and I was also eager to jump back into my training.

One day soon after, Henry and I were having a tough tennis workout. He was feeding me balls from his huge basket. My job was to run my hardest and hit the ball crosscourt. Then he would quickly feed another ball to the opposite side of the court. This was meant to improve my ability to hit on the run, which is important in tennis. It was really tiring. At one point I stopped, choosing to grab a quick rest.

Henry stopped for a moment and said, "Bryan, I know you're exhausted. But *never* give up. Learn to make the extra effort every single time."

I sighed. "What do you do when your body says 'no more'?"

"Tell it to shut up." Henry smiled. "Obviously, everyone gets to that point eventually. Still, you've got to believe in yourself. You can always reach down and find the energy to stay out there for a few more games. I really want you to develop that attitude. It'll help you win an important match one day, I guarantee it."

"All right, Henry," I said, taking a deep breath and getting in the ready position again.

"Good, kid. Okay, let's switch gears for now. We'll pick up where we left off yesterday with your second serve."

I threw my arms up in the air and joked, "Not

the second serve *again*!"

Henry laughed. We had been spending a great deal of time on it recently. He felt it was one of the most important shots in tennis.

"Bryan, let me tell you a story about the legendary Sam 'Grand Slam' Diamond. Have I ever told you about the conversation I had with him?"

He had, many times. But I remembered Mrs. Johnson's advice about pretending every story was brand new. "I don't think so," I said.

"He was one of the top servers in the 1940's. Even if he were down love-40 on his serve, he would still be favored to win the game—against anybody in the world! Once, I asked him what made his serve so effective. To my surprise, he talked about—"

"His second serve!" I interrupted with a laugh, finishing Henry's story, "He could always go for broke on his first serve. If he missed, he still had a great second serve to fall back on."

Henry chuckled. "I guess you *have* heard that one before. I remember it like it was yesterday. 'Grand Slam' looked right at me. He said, 'Henry, as far as I'm concerned, *you're only as good as your second serve.*' I've never forgotten that statement."

At the end of September, I participated in the Oklahoma State Fall Junior Open. This was a very important step for me. It marked the first time I had ever traveled out of Kansas to play tennis. These "sectional tournaments" were very tough because they didn't only include junior players from Kansas. They also included juniors from some other states in my "section" of the country. As a result, the level of competition was much higher. I lost in the first round, but it was a close match. My second sectional tournament was the Midtown Junior Fall Classic, in the state of Iowa. Once again, I played well but fell in the first round. Despite the fact that I lost in both tournaments, Henry was happy with the way I'd played.

"These experiences are gonna be good for your game, kid."

"Yeah, but I lost to guys who aren't even national players. They're not even the best players in my section."

"I know, Bryan, but you'll get there. The top kids are obviously a couple of levels above you right now. Still, I think you're going to be surprised how quickly you can close the gap. The important thing is that you've started playing sectional tournaments."

"I guess," I said, "but it's so frustrating because I had a chance to win both of those matches. If I'd just played a couple of points better, who knows what might have happened?"

"There's a very fine line between winning and losing in tennis. That reminds me of an expression that always helped Johnny in tight matches. I would tell him: 'The game that gets you there won't win it for you.' Do you understand what that means?"

I scratched my head, "Not really."

"It's pretty simple," Henry explained. "Great

players always seem to play their best when the pressure is on, right?"

"Sure, that's what makes them so tough."

"Exactly. And you have to do that too. As a matter of fact, you have to do *better* than that. When a match is very close, you have to raise your game to the next level. That's the only way to close out a big match against that type of player."

Now I understood. "Great players step it up when they have to. If I don't raise my game in close matches, I'm gonna lose because the other guy *will* raise his game."

"That's why the superstars almost always get the close ones. In big-time tennis, you have to *win* the match, Bryan. Nobody is going to hand it to you. You have to go for it all."

One night in late November, I sat at my desk reviewing my upcoming schedule. There were two important sectional tournaments coming up. One was the Junior Holiday Classic, held in Missouri, in December. The other was the Winter Classic, held in Oklahoma, in early February. I had already proven that I could win in my own state. Now I was hoping for my first win in sectional play in one of these tournaments.

There was one other date that was highlighted boldly on my calendar. January 15 marked the return of my favorite tournament, the Courage Open. It always came around just a few days after my birthday, making it special. I was turning sixteen, a very meaningful birthday for a kid who was looking forward to getting his driver's license!

In addition, the tournament would give me an opportunity to realize a dream. I had something to prove to everybody in Courage, Kansas. I wanted them to see what a great coach—and great friend—I had in old Henry Johnson.

CHAPTER SEVEN

THE RETURN OF THE COURAGE OPEN

The improvement in my tennis had been noticed by The Courts' tournament committee. They had seeded me fourth in the Courage Open. That made me proud, but I was aware that it placed added pressure on my shoulders. For the first time ever, people were looking at me with high expectations.

On January 15, I walked up the stairs to the huge lounge at nine o'clock in the morning. I smiled when I saw Mrs. Fletcher at the desk. Good ol' Mrs. Fletcher! She gave me a big smile.

"Well, here we are again, Bryan."

"Yep. And I'm hoping to go a lot further than I did last year."

"I hope so, too."

My first round was a breeze because my opponent, Larry Cooper, wasn't very good. Things got tougher later on when I faced Bill Foster in the second round, but I was in a groove. When Foster served, I moved in and caught the returns early. I hit the ball at his feet time and time again. He was known as an effective serve-and-volley player, but he was no match for my new game. I won easily, 6-2, 6-1.

"Bryan, you were wonderful today!" My mom embarrassed me with a big hug as I came up the stairs. Dad gave me a predictable pat on the back. Henry offered his usual, "Good work, kid."

I was pleased that a successful day of tennis was behind me. Mom went home to start dinner, while Dad and I went to Brandon's basketball game. I had a good feeling about my next match the following day. I believed that I was too powerful for my opponent, Keith Nichols. If I won, that would put me in the quarterfinals for the first time ever. As an added bonus, I would probably be facing an opponent who I knew *very* well—Ted Grover. He was playing good tennis, and looked like a sure bet to reach the quarters. We were on a collision course with one another.

The next morning I was back in action against Keith Nichols, a good baseline player. I had expected a slightly tighter match, but to my surprise I marched into the quarterfinals in a rout, 6-3, 6-1. Henry was waiting for me when I came up the stairs.

"Good work, kid, you looked sharp out there. How do you feel?"

"I feel great, Henry. Ready to play another match."

Henry laughed, "I'm glad to hear that, because Ted Grover also won his third-round match. It's you and him at two o'clock. Everybody's already talking about it."

Just like that, I had to face off against the biggest jerk in Courage once again. A few short hours later, I found myself warming up on court number one with Ted Grover. I was nervous, but also very excited. Grover, on the other hand, seemed strangely quiet. He knew that a large crowd was watching from the lounge upstairs. He also knew he wasn't playing the same kid he'd beaten a year earlier. Among other things, I now stood close to six-feet-tall. I had grown several inches during the past twelve months, just like Dad had predicted. That made me very happy, and it felt like I wasn't even done growing.

As we finished our warm-ups, I was ready to play. Last year, Grover had taken advantage of my flat forehand and shaky serve. Fortunately, those strokes had been replaced. I had also gotten much stronger because of Henry's training. Of course, the biggest difference between this year and last year was just having Henry as a friend. After everything he'd taught me, I was ready to face off against Ted Grover.

As the quarterfinals of the Courage Open got under way, the spectators thought they were going to be watching a tight battle. That's not the way it ended up. When Grover came to the net, my passing shots flew by him. When he rallied from the baseline, my accurate groundstrokes left him flat-footed. When he tried to hit passing shots, I hit crisp volley winners from the net. As always, Grover made some cheating line calls. He also tried to intimidate me. But this was not last year. This time, his behavior only made him look like a fool. And when the crowd started booing him, I couldn't help but smile.

Losing to Ted Grover last year had been a crushing experience. It had taken countless hours of hard work, but I finally got my revenge. I approached the match like it was the finals of Wimbledon. Playing with determination, I destroyed him 6-1, 6-0.

The final point of the match was especially sweet. I was toying with Grover, hitting the ball softly to keep the rally going. I was waiting for something I could really clobber. After we had exchanged about ten balls, Grover tried to hit a winner up my forehand line. I got there in a flash. With the topspin forehand that Henry had taught me, I battered that ball. I hit it so hard that a beaten-down Grover didn't even try for it. He just stood and stared for a second. Now that the match was complete, I raised my fist and let out a loud yell. I had nothing more to say to Grover—I think he got the message! I glanced up to the lounge, where people were congratulating Henry. That made me feel great.

A little while later, I was finally able to spend a few minutes alone with Henry. We were both excited because I was now in the semifinals of the Courage

Open. *The semis.* That had a nice ring to it. Before leaving with my family, I reached into my tennis bag. Fishing out an envelope, I handed it to Henry. It was a gift I'd made on my computer for him.

Henry opened it carefully. The front was a drawing of two people, an older man and a teenager. They were standing in front of a building with a sign that said "The Courts." They were both smiling and holding tennis rackets. I made it look similar to the old photo of Henry and Johnny standing together. When Henry opened up the card, he found the following words:

Dear Henry,

I've never said a proper thank you for all the things you do for me. Your encouragement gives me the strength to work hard every day. It's difficult to imagine what type of tennis player I would have been if not for you. So I want to say thanks. I also want to explain why I'm giving you this card today. I mean, I know it's not your birthday. But do you remember what happened a year ago on this very day? That's when I lost to Ted Grover and you came over and talked to me for the very first time. You started teaching me stuff right away. That's a day I'll always remember.

Your friend,

Bryan

The next weekend, the four remaining players gathered at The Courts for the semifinals. I had hoped that Jimmy would be among them. Unfortunately, he had been defeated in the quarters. I felt bad for him, but I had problems of my own. My opponent was the greatest player in the history of Courage, Mike Scully! I had always dreamed of a moment like this, but now that it was here, I was very nervous.

This was by far the most attention I had ever received at The Courts. More than fifty spectators were lined up around court number one. There was also an overflowing crowd in the lounge upstairs. People wanted to see me take on the defending champion.

I had spent the last couple of hours with Henry, relaxing and talking quietly. The old man was trying to keep me from getting too nervous. After going over the game plan, he handed me a piece of paper. It was folded over a couple of times. "What's this?" I asked, puzzled.

"It's nothing, Bryan, don't even think about it. Just stick it in your pocket. You can take a quick peek at it after the first set. Now, let's go over strategy again."

When it was time for our match, Scully greeted me warmly at the desk. As we walked down to court one, I was more nervous than ever before. Realizing this, Scully made some friendly small talk to help ease the tension. He said, "Nice job getting to the semis. You sure let Grover have it. He got what he deserved!" Scully's words made me feel good and I relaxed a little.

As we were warming up, I tried to forget about all the people who were watching. Instead, I concentrated on hitting the ball smoothly. But when Scully prepared to serve, I suddenly felt nervous all over again. As the match began, I missed four straight returns. We switched sides and Scully quickly broke my serve to make it 2-love.

By the time I was serving at love-5, I wasn't even sure what to do. I felt powerless as Scully continued to hit fantastic shots with ease. Just like that, the first set was over, 6-0. It had taken barely twenty minutes for the bagel to be served up.

Scully held serve easily to open the second set. I started to walk to the other side of the court to change ends. As I did, I glanced up at Henry, who was watching from the lounge upstairs. He was motioning to his pocket and then pointing at me. The piece of paper! I had forgotten all about it. Slipping it out of my pocket, I unfolded the paper and looked at it. One sentence only was printed in Henry's handwriting: *"If you're afraid to lose, you can't win."*

As I slowly picked up a ball and prepared to serve, I gazed at Henry. The old man nodded. The message was clear: win or lose, it was time to stop playing scared. It was time to play *my* style of aggressive, confident tennis. I couldn't help but smile for a second. I thought to myself: *That old man is so smart!* He always seemed to know when I was going to be in trouble, and how to get me back on track.

Tossing the ball high up in the air, I blasted a serve right down the center. The fast pace caught Scully off guard. Still, he was talented enough to flick a one-handed backhand deep in the court. I slid over to my left and looped my two-handed backhand crosscourt. Scully was there, slicing a backhand and rushing to the net. I anticipated it perfectly, lifting an offensive topspin lob that was just beyond his reach. It landed softly right on the baseline. The crowd cheered and I pumped my fist. *Now we're talkin'!*

All of a sudden, the match changed dramatically. To this point, Scully had been winning easily. However, he could not ignore the fact that this had turned into a *real* tennis match. The action continued without pause until we were deadlocked at 6-all. I had forced Mike Scully into a tiebreaker! The second set was nearly an hour old.

The crowd was enjoying this match, cheering loudly with every great shot. Scully, an aggressive player, was always looking for an opportunity to get to the net. Now that I was hitting the ball with more accuracy, it wasn't as easy for him to attack. When we both stayed back on the baseline, the points were long and exciting.

During the tiebreaker, the level of tennis didn't

fade. Mike Scully obviously knew how to handle pressure. On the other hand, I was still learning. At 3-all, Scully raised his game to a higher level. Suddenly, he was hitting the ball with even more power. I didn't ease up, but Scully drew on all of his experience as a former pro player. He played the last four points like a champion. He overwhelmed me, winning the tiebreaker, 7-3, and the match, 6-0, 7-6.

The game that gets you there won't win it for you. This was one of Henry's favorite expressions, and now I *really* understood what it meant. Mike Scully had skillfully demonstrated it—like all great players, he had raised his game in the most important part of the match. I knew Henry was thrilled that I had received this real-life tournament lesson. Now that I had actually seen it up close, hopefully I would be able to do it myself one day.

When I shook hands with Mike at the net, I was smiling. I knew this had been a very valuable experience. It was satisfying to realize that all those long hours were starting to pay off. Henry had given me the ultimate compliment recently. He had told me that my dedication to tennis was similar to one other kid— Johnny Matthews. He also choked up when he thanked me for the card. He said it was something he would treasure until the day he died.

A word of praise from Mike Scully was like icing on the cake, "Bryan, that was incredible! When I saw you play Grover, I knew you had improved. But to tell you the truth, I took you lightly. Until today, I

didn't realize how good you'd gotten."
   Until this day, neither did I.

CHAPTER EIGHT

PREPARING FOR BATTLE

One night in late May, I sat at my computer after finishing my homework. The house was quiet and I had the radio on softly. I was reflecting upon the fast pace of the last few months. Henry and I had been working harder than ever, shooting for our goal— a chance to go to the nationals.

As the number two ranked sixteen-year-old player in Kansas, my confidence level was high. Still, I had a tough road ahead of me. First, I would have to compete against the best players from my section, which included five states—Iowa, Nebraska, Kansas, Oklahoma, and Missouri. This was the pressure-packed Missouri Valley Supers Circuit that I had missed last summer because of my injury. Basically, it was a three-week series of tournaments only for highly ranked juniors. Based on the results of these three tournaments, a selection committee would choose six kids to move on to the nationals. Only *six kids*...out of five states! They would join other kids from across the country that had also been chosen to move on to the nationals. These juniors—America's finest—would come together to compete at several famous national championship tournaments.

Thinking about battling the best players from my section was both exciting and scary. The stakes at the Missouri Valley Supers Circuit simply couldn't be any higher—and there was one other thing that added to the pressure. After the first two tournaments, only sixteen players would advance to the third tournament. The selection committee would use the results from the first two tournaments to choose the top sixteen kids. This would set the stage for the single most important sectional event of the year, the Missouri Valley "Sweet Sixteen" tournament. If you weren't in this tournament, you had no chance to go to the nationals.

I felt ready. I was healthy, and I was hitting the ball better than ever. I had lots of good players to train with, including my best friend, Jimmy. Playing against him was great practice. Although I had recently moved past him in tennis, he was still a very gifted athlete. Our matches were perfect preparation for the tournaments that lay just ahead.

There was only one thing I was bummed out about. Henry had come down with a bad case of the flu. He was stuck in bed at home. When I visited him, he didn't want to talk about his illness. As always, he insisted on putting my tennis first. The Missouri Valley Supers Circuit was only a week away, and I needed some help. The old man instructed me to call Mike Scully. Ever since our match at the Courage Open, Mike had shown an interest in my tennis. Still, I had doubts about calling him.

"Henry, you and I have been together for a year and a half. I don't know if I can be out there working with Mike, or anybody else."

"Bryan," Henry stated, "we've done a lot of work together. These are big goals we're shooting for. This is the time for you to play your best tennis. I wish I didn't have this stupid flu right now. But whether I'm in the stands watching, or resting at home, I'm with you."

"Okay, Henry, whatever you say. But Mike's a busy guy. I don't know if he'll even want to help me train for these tournaments."

"I think you're gonna be surprised, kid."

As usual, Henry's gut feeling was right on the money. Upon hearing about the situation, Mike Scully agreed to help me out. He said he was happy to help out a fellow "player." That made me feel really good. So with Mike on board, I was able to continue training at a high level.

The following Saturday, I walked into the clubhouse of the Oklahoma City Tennis Center. I could feel the electricity in the air. I stared at all the great players that had gathered here. The best kids from five states! All of us were ready to begin the Missouri Valley Supers Circuit. The most important three weeks of the year had arrived.

"Drew Phillips, Bryan Berry, report to the tournament desk please." It was time. My opponent and I were given a can of balls, and then we walked out to court four. Drew Phillips, the seventh seed, was scary because of his size—190 pounds of sheer muscle on a six-foot-two-inch frame. His game was extremely dangerous. He was a big hitter who wasn't afraid to aim for the lines.

I had been nervous all day thinking about this match. However, as we started warming up, I felt pretty relaxed. When Phillips held up a ball indicating that he was ready to serve, I nodded. I blocked everything else out of my mind. He tossed the ball into the air and swung—the tournament was under way! I was able to catch the ball early and return his serve with a strong shot. It forced Phillips out of position. All he could do was reach out and punch the ball toward the middle of the court. It landed softly at shoulder height. I ran over and hit my topspin forehand crosscourt for a clean winner. *Thanks Henry!* A shaky forehand that broke down under pressure was long gone. It had been replaced with a powerful stroke that I could always rely on.

The tennis was high quality, with neither of us backing down. But I seemed to have an answer on all the crucial points. When the dust settled, I had racked up a convincing, 7-5, 6-4, victory. I couldn't remember ever hitting the ball so well. I was beaming with satisfaction as I walked back to report the score. I did belong here with all these excellent tennis players! All my doubts seemed to fade away with this one solid performance. I now knew that I could compete with anybody in my section. I couldn't wait to get back out on the court and prove it.

I fought my way to the quarterfinals before finally falling. I lost a tough three-setter to the number two seed, Billy Richardson. It was a great match that seesawed back and forth until the very end. With growing confidence, I returned to Courage determined to keep the momentum going. All I needed was one more good tournament. That would certainly place me among the top sixteen players. Then I'd be invited to play the all-important Missouri Valley Sweet Sixteen tournament. I eagerly looked forward to the next event. Mike Scully and I worked hard to prepare for it. I reported each night to Henry, who was still struggling with his illness. I found out that when an elderly person gets sick, it takes much longer to recover.

Six days later I was in the state of Iowa for the second tournament. After an easy first-round victory, I faced Craig Schroeder of Missouri. He was a terrific baseline player who came into this second-round match as the fifth seed. A short, skinny kid, Schroeder neither served hard nor attacked the net. He didn't make very many mistakes either. He had displayed his skill the previous week by battling his way to the semis.

Schroeder was a very tough opponent, and he made me work for every point. Winning a baseline rally against him required great concentration. Luckily, I felt strong even after two hours had gone by. Those long practices with the old man were definitely paying off.

I had to deal with many challenges in this match. The most difficult one was facing a match point! After dropping the first set, I was serving at 4-5, 30-40, in the second set. Beads of sweat dripped down my forehead and splashed onto the court. This was what I had trained for. I went for a big first serve, hoping for an ace. Unfortunately, it caught the net and fell back on my own side. Breathing deeply, I tossed the ball high into the air. This was the most crucial second serve of my entire life. If I double faulted here, the match was over! Thank goodness I had worked so hard with Henry on my second serve.

I hit it perfectly. The ball traveled through the air with enough spin to easily clear the net. Schroeder returned the ball, setting off another long baseline rally. I was waiting and hoping for a good opportunity. A few moments later, my patience was finally rewarded. Schroeder hit a backhand that landed a little short. With no hesitation whatsoever, I pounded the ball crosscourt and charged the net. Out of position, Schroeder tried to pass me up the line. I was right there for the easy winner. Whew! I had survived a match point. Relieved, I went on a hot streak. When it ended, I had the biggest win of my life, 3-6, 7-5, 6-4.

I had taken out the fifth seed!

Later that evening I thought about my situation. With my win today, I'd already beaten a couple of quality players. I had a very positive feeling that I was going to earn an invitation to the Missouri Valley Sweet Sixteen tournament. If so, fifteen other players and I would come together for one final battle. Six players would then be selected to play at the nationals. This was something I wanted more than anything else in the world. I guess I was even surprising myself. I had no idea I would be able to compete with these guys.

Maybe I was overconfident, because the next day was a disaster. I just couldn't get anything going. Eric Davis, the number four seed, destroyed me, 6-1, 6-2. I felt slow and weak during this lousy performance. Of course, this bad loss filled my head with some serious doubts. I wondered: *Will this wipe away the good things I've already done?*

I was pretty anxious when I spoke to Henry on the phone that night. He calmed me down, telling me not to focus on this one bad day. I had proven that I could play with the best players from my section. My fate was now in the hands of the selection committee.

Henry wasn't too worried. I had beaten some solid players over the last couple of weeks. Most of them would probably end up at the Missouri Valley Sweet Sixteen tournament. He felt sure that I would be chosen among the top sixteen.

I got the news the next morning. My parents, Brandon, and I were hanging out at our hotel. We were packing up our things and getting ready to check out. When the phone rang, I leaped at it. It was Mr. Jenkins from the selection committee. Wanting a little privacy, I took the phone into the bathroom. After we spoke briefly, I hung up and walked back into the room. I lowered my eyes and cast a sad glance at Brandon and my parents. They were totally shocked. Dad stood up to give me another pat on the back, but I dodged him. Then I cracked a big smile as I playfully grabbed Brandon. "Just kidding, bro, I'm in!" An hour later we were back on the road to Courage. My dream was still alive.

CHAPTER NINE

THE FINAL PIECE OF THE PUZZLE

After dropping off my stuff at home, I wasted no time getting over to Henry's house. When I walked through his front door, he was sitting on the sofa. He was covered in a thick blanket, with the newspaper on his lap.

"Hey Henry, how are you feeling?"

"Like an old man. How are you, kid?" He smiled broadly. "Ready to play the Sweet Sixteen tournament?"

"I don't know…it just doesn't seem real. It almost feels like a dream. I keep waiting for someone to wake me."

"This is no dream," the old man replied, speaking through a heavy cough. "Didn't I always tell you the hard work would pay off?"

I laughed, joking, "I don't remember, Henry. All I can remember is you always yelling at me to work harder!" I spent the next hour telling him about the tournament. Then, although I was having a great time, I got up to leave. I knew he needed to rest.

During the following five days, I trained with Mike Scully. He was helping me to prepare for the big tournament. Henry was smart to put us together, and Mike had quickly become a trusted friend. The old man was pleased to see Mike take such an active role. He felt that I could learn a great deal from the former pro player. Obviously, nobody could replace Henry, but unfortunately he was still sick at home.

When I arrived at the Wichita Tennis Club, I was downright nervous. I had been dreaming about the nationals for years. Now I was one of only sixteen kids who had a chance. This tournament was the final piece of the puzzle.

My opponent was the number six seed, Peter Campbell. He was a lefty with a powerful game. Campbell, the number two player in Nebraska, seemed to have only one weak spot, his slice backhand. I figured it out after he blasted a couple of forehand winners. Then he hit a forehand winner off my biggest first serve. That's when I realized that I had to change up my game plan. If not, I'd be hitting the showers early. *Man, does this guy have a monster forehand!*

Taking a moment to adjust the strings on my racket, I tried to think. What had Henry taught me about this type of player? I suddenly remembered. *A big hitter loves a fast pace.* Henry always said that guys who hit the ball hard liked it when you hit it hard to them. They could just feed off your power. He compared it to a baseball slugger who loves fastballs, but has trouble with curves. I realized that Peter Campbell was that type of player. I knew what Henry would want me to do: *ease up a little bit and make him create his own power!*

So that's what I did. At love-15, I hit a spin serve to Campbell's backhand. All he could do was slice the ball weakly over the net. Instead of trying to pound a winner, I hit it deep to his backhand again. He returned it, but he was clearly uncomfortable with the slower pace. When I went back to his backhand for the third time, his slice attempt was too low. This time it caught the net and fell back to his side. I continued to use this strategy, and it definitely made a difference. Sure, a few times Campbell hit a huge forehand. Other than that, I was completely in control. My plan was successful, wearing the lefty down. The match went my way, 7-5, 7-5.

Mike Scully, who was sitting in the stands, was extremely pleased. "That was great, Bryan. You found his weakness and you took advantage of it."

The next day I went up against the third seed, Ricky Segal of Iowa. Segal had been chosen the previous year to move on to the nationals—so this was a guy who already had experience at the national level. A win over him would be huge.

It was a terrific match. Segal won the first set, 7-6, 10-8 in the tiebreaker. I fought back, refusing to go down. I won the second set, 6-4. Then we played to the wire in the third set—another tiebreaker.

Before the start of the deciding tiebreaker, I exchanged glances with Mike Scully. He was sitting in the stands looking at me and pumping his fist. He was trying to give me the confidence to go for it. That made me remember our tiebreaker at the Courage Open. Mike's incredible performance that day had taught me one of Henry's favorite lessons: *The game that gets you there won't win it for you.*

On the opening point of the tiebreaker, I returned Segal's serve and charged directly to the net. He must have been shocked, because I hadn't done that once in the entire match. He responded with a high topspin lob. I jumped in the air and *wham!* I pounded an overhead winner. Getting the opening point of the tiebreaker was important for me. I stayed aggressive, riding the momentum to the most exciting victory of my career. The score in the tiebreaker ended up being 7-2. The match was mine, 7-6 in the third.

When I walked off the court, I felt really good. Mike and I bumped knuckles, and a lot of people were coming up to congratulate me. It was an awesome experience. However, even while I was celebrating my biggest win ever, part of me was sad. It was never far from my mind that someone was missing. It just didn't feel right. *Henry, if only you could have been here to see this.*

But there was something I didn't know. While I had been battling on the court, Henry was engaged in a battle for his *life*. That very same day, a major turn of events had happened. Henry Johnson, an old man who meant the world to me, had suffered a heart attack. Everything was about to change.

When I got home that afternoon, I found the message on my answering machine. It was from Elizabeth Johnson, who was over at the hospital. I rushed right over. When I found her, she was talking quietly to a nurse. Elizabeth turned to me as I approached, hugging me tightly. "Thanks for coming, Bryan." Her face was pale and she looked very upset. "Henry didn't want you to know until after you played your match."

"What happened?"

"It was about six this morning," Elizabeth said. "Henry tried to get up to go to the bathroom. Suddenly, I heard him fall to the floor. I called 911 and they rushed him straight to the hospital."

I asked fearfully, "Will he...will he be okay?"

Elizabeth looked at me for a long moment. "Bryan, they're not sure. He's very sick. Remember, Henry is eighty-four years old."

I knew how old Henry was, although sometimes it was the easiest thing in the world to forget. He was more than a coach, he was a true friend. I never really thought about how old he was. His energy and strength made him seem so young.

"Can I see him?" The nurse frowned, but Elizabeth looked at me and smiled. "Go ahead, Bryan. I know that old man. Talking to you about tennis will be better medicine than anything this hospital can give him."

She was right. Henry didn't even give me a chance to say anything. His face was tired and weak, but his eyes lit up when he saw me. In a hoarse voice that was close to a whisper, he asked, "How'd you do in your match?"

"Henry," I replied, "I won it for you today, 7-6 in the third over the number three seed. We're in the semis." I could see the satisfaction in his face. Although Henry could barely keep his eyes open, this made him very happy. I touched his hand just before I left, and he smiled at me.

The next day I was back at the tournament facing the top seed, Cory Marshall. He was the number one sixteen-year-old in the whole section. Marshall was truly a skilled player. He produced some amazing tennis, beating me, 7-5, 6-4.

Two nights later I was sitting in Henry's hospital room, feeling sad. The three weeks of the Missouri Valley Supers Circuit was finally over. In a couple of days, the sectional office would announce which six kids they had chosen to move on to the nationals. I wasn't even thinking about that right now. I just hoped that Henry could get back out on the court one day. I would have gladly traded every win of my life for that to happen. But with each passing day, his recovery seemed less likely.

I looked around the small room. Elizabeth had brightened it up with some flowers and balloons. My homemade gift was an old tennis racket, which I had decorated. I painted tennis balls with happy faces and glued them onto the racket. Then I spread a banner across it that read "Get well, Henry."

"You're quiet tonight, kid. Everything all right?"

"Yeah, I'm just a little tired."

"Well, you've got a right to be. You've played a lot of tennis these last couple of weeks. I'm proud of you." Even while facing his illness, Henry seemed to be in good spirits.

"Do you think it will be enough to get us over the top?"

Henry smiled weakly. That question had been on our minds all day. "Until we hear which six kids they're sending to the nationals, all we can do is wait."

"That's harder than actually playing the tennis."

Henry chuckled, "You can say that again. But look, you did well in every tournament. You also beat a couple of the best players. I think you have a shot to make it."

The next day lasted forever. I would find out the results the following morning. On Henry's advice, I took the day off from tennis to give my tired body a rest. I was able to distract myself by hanging out with my friends and going to a movie. By bedtime, I was too nervous to fall asleep. In a few short hours I would know if I was going to the nationals. This was something I had dreamed about for many years. Yet, while it was so close, it wasn't my main concern anymore. My friend Henry was very old and very sick. I tried not to think about it, but I had to wonder: What was going to happen? I feared that the end was near.

The next morning, I made the call to the sectional office as soon as I woke up. By ten o'clock, I arrived at the hospital, where Henry and Elizabeth were talking softly. She had already been there for several hours. We all chatted for a few minutes, and then Elizabeth got up to get a cup of coffee from the hospital cafeteria.

Henry didn't say a word. He just looked at me and waited. His eyes burned with the intensity that I had grown so used to. He had worked every bit as hard as I had over the past couple of years. I sometimes joked that Henry had even outworked me.

I had typed and printed out the final ruling of the committee. My title for the page was "Boys' Sixteens." Without a word I held the list in front of Henry's face:

1. Cory Marshall
2. Billy Richardson
3. Ricky Segal
4. Eric Davis
5. Craig Schroeder
6. Bryan Berry

Henry was silent for a moment, overcome with emotion. Then he whispered, "You did it, kid."

"*We* did it, Henry."

"I guess we did, Bryan, and this is only the beginning for you." The old man smiled weakly, joking, "I'm sure Ted Grover will be pleased to hear the good news."

"Ted *who*?" I responded with a straight face. Henry laughed softly.

We started to talk about my plans for the rest of the summer, but Henry's eyes kept closing. He was exhausted. Finally he sighed, "Bryan, I want to talk to you but I'm just too tired right now. Come back later, kid."

I met Mike Scully at The Courts a couple of hours later. When I told him the news about the nationals, he couldn't have been more excited. He said it was like living his dreams all over again. I was happy and grateful that Mike was now a part of my team. We did some practice drills and then played three tough sets. When we finished, I did my exercises and took a shower. Then I went back to the hospital to visit Henry. For some reason, I had a nervous feeling inside.

CHAPTER TEN

FROM COURAGE TO KALAMAZOO

Henry had barely touched his dinner when I walked in. Elizabeth was worried, because she wanted him to keep his strength up. Still, she managed a smile. "Just a few minutes tonight. All right, guys?" She walked out of the room, giving us some time to be alone. I sat down in the chair by the bed. Before Henry spoke, he coughed and struggled for breath, which worried me. However, his face looked happy. He stared right at me and said, "Bryan, I'm so proud of you. Your tennis has come such a long way. What makes you special is how much you truly love the game. I never met anyone who loved tennis the way Johnny did—until I met you." Henry took another breath before finishing his thought. "You've worked hard and you deserve your success, Bryan. Remember what I once told you? It's a long way from Courage to Kalamazoo. Well, kid, you've earned your ticket."

"I'm scared, Henry. It's a whole new ball game now."

"You wouldn't be human if you weren't scared." The old man was choosing his words carefully. "You'll be playing some true superstars at the national tournaments. You just have to believe in your heart that you're every bit as good as they are." He looked deep into my eyes and told me, "At first, there might be some difficult matches that shake your confidence. But keep your head up, because you *do* belong with them."

"Okay, Henry, I hear you."

"Good, kid. Look, I can't predict how long it will take you to reach their level. It might take one match, or maybe the whole summer. But I can assure you of one thing. There's going to be a time when it all comes together for you. And when it happens, don't question it. Just go with it. It's like a surfer riding a wave. You ride it as long and as far as you can."

The door opened and Elizabeth walked in. She looked at Henry and said, "It's time for you to rest."

"Soon, Elizabeth. I need to talk to the kid just a little while longer." She sighed, and then smiled, "You'll never change, will you?"

"Too late to change now."

She looked at us and said, "Fifteen more minutes." Then she walked out of the room.

"Bryan, pour me some water, please." Filling a

cup from the pitcher by the bed, I put it to Henry's lips. He drank a small amount. "Thanks, kid." He struggled mightily to clear his throat enough to speak. "Listen, no matter what happens, hang in there and don't get discouraged. Don't let these guys intimidate you just because they're national players. I want you to get out there and lay it all on the line."

Henry paused. I could see that speaking was very hard for him. I started to suggest that we call it a night, but he waved me off. "I'm fine. Now, in August, when you get to Kalamazoo, I want you to do something for me. I want you introduce yourself to one of my oldest friends. He's a fellow by the name of Charlie Morrison. He's there every year and you'll have no trouble finding him. Tell him I said hello, will you please?"

"Sure, Henry." My eyes started to get watery. "Anyway, you'll be there with me by then. You can say hello to him yourself."

Henry smiled gently, "I don't think so, kid." Tears filled up in my eyes. I felt Henry's hand squeezing mine. I moved closer to him. The old man smiled weakly and looked up at me. "Don't be sad, Bryan. This last year and a half has been amazing. I wouldn't trade it for anything in the world. As you know, I'm fond of saying that you're only as good as your second serve. Coaching you, well, it was *my* second serve...my second chance." The old man looked into my eyes and said, "Everything makes sense to me now."

A few tears rolled down my cheeks. I was having trouble speaking, but Henry didn't seem to care. He was just happy that we were together. After a little while, he patted me on the hand and whispered, "All right, Bryan, you should be getting on home."

"Okay, Henry. I'll come back tomorrow." As I turned and walked toward the door, I was overcome with emotion. Somehow, I knew at that exact moment that I would never see Henry again. My eyes filled with more tears. As my hand touched the doorknob, I turned around to look at him one last time. The old man was staring right at me with a gentle, peaceful expression. Then he slowly held out his hand. I rushed over to the bed and hugged my coach. I was crying openly now.

"It's okay, kid. Everything's going to work out for you, you'll see."

"Henry, I want to tell you th…that—" I was trying to find the right words.

"It's all right, Bryan, I know exactly what you want to say. Oh my, you remind me so much of Johnny. You wanna know something, kid? I never got over the hurt of losing him until you came along. For fifty years I've felt bad that I never had a chance to tell him just one thing. I don't want to miss this chance with you." Henry paused. "I love you, Bryan."

The funeral was a week later. I cried, as did Elizabeth, but it was comforting to have the chance to say a final goodbye to Henry. I thought about canceling my plans for the summer, but my parents encouraged me to go forward. They knew that losing Henry was something I would never get over. Still, they told me that it was okay to move on with my life. I knew that Henry would want it that way.

Henry had been smart to warn me about not getting discouraged. My first two national tournaments ended quickly. I got beaten badly by far more experienced players. Finally, in my third tournament, I won a match. I defeated a kid from South Carolina, 6-3 in the third set. It was satisfying to get my first victory in national competition. Unfortunately, I quickly fell in the second round, 6-2, 6-3. But I was starting to find my groove. In the next tournament, I won two matches before losing.

Things went ahead as scheduled. At the end of July, my family and I hit the road to the state of Michigan. Kalamazoo was my fifth national tournament. It was the city of the "National Championships." This was the oldest and most important junior tennis tournament in America.

When we arrived, we checked in at our hotel. A sign on the wall read: "Welcome to Kalamazoo, host of the National Championships for over fifty years." I felt a shiver run down my spine. Henry's words entered my mind: *"It's a long way from Courage to Kalamazoo."*

Two days later, I was so nervous I thought I was going to be sick. Just one short year ago I had been playing small tournaments in Kansas. Now I was playing my first match ever at the National Championships! Right after my first serve of the day, my nerves calmed down. This is what Henry and I had worked for. Suddenly, I was ready to play.

Joe Drucker, my opponent, was very tough. He was a lefty with an excellent serve and volley. The kid from Berkeley, California, was giving me a tremendous challenge. But something strange happened early in the match that changed everything. We were deadlocked at 3-all in a tight first set. I had just earned my first break point as a result of a missed forehand by Drucker. He was down 30-40. Drucker rushed to the net behind a wide serve that pulled me off the court. I hit a backhand return that stayed up in the air just a little too long. Drucker hit a sharp crosscourt volley that seemed to be out of my reach. At that instant I had an amazing experience. I wondered if my imagination was playing tricks on me. It suddenly felt like I was back home in Courage playing a practice match. As always, Henry would be watching from his spot in the lounge upstairs. He would be yelling, clapping, and motivating me. He believed in giving effort on every single point. *If I don't chase that ball down, Henry's never gonna let me forget it!*

Without hesitation I started running for the ball. I couldn't quite get there in time, so I did something crazy. I jumped and lunged at the ball—the way a third baseman dives to stop a rocket down the line. In mid-air, I swung as hard as I could. To my surprise, I nailed a topspin forehand right up the line. It was just beyond Drucker's reach. He stood there shocked. Actually, I was a little shocked myself. It was the greatest shot that had ever exploded off my racket.

When that happened, a change immediately took place. I *knew* that I belonged here. Henry often talked about a moment that would prove that I had made it to the big-time. He said it might be a single point, or even just one shot. I was sure that I had just experienced that special moment. The old man had given me the confidence to shoot for the stars.

My new attitude carried me through to 6-4, 6-3, victory. The win broke the ice for me. It was important because it was intimidating just being at Kalamazoo. There were some players in this tournament who were very well known. The top seed, Danny Gold, was the best player by far—but the top four or five guys were all incredible. They were simply the most talented sixteen-year-olds in America.

None of that mattered anymore. I stopped thinking about who was famous, or who was seeded. Henry had taught me to live in the moment, and that's what I was doing. I was hitting the ball as well as anyone there. Nobody in the tournament had a stronger desire to win. It was helpful that I now had four national tournaments under my belt. The experience I had gained was teaching me how to win at this level. True, I wasn't a famous junior like Danny Gold. As a matter of fact, I was just an unknown kid from the state of Kansas.

But I was peaking at exactly the right time.

CHAPTER ELEVEN

KALAMAZOO

The next day, I defeated Michael Anderson of Los Angeles, California, 6-2 in the third set. Although the conditions were hot and humid, both of us were up to the challenge. Anderson only stood about five-foot-eight, but he was a solid baseliner who hit with two hands off both sides. After the first two sets were decided by tiebreakers, I pulled ahead. I simply overpowered Anderson with my strength.

That evening I was on the phone with Mike Scully, who was back in Courage. I told him all about my match with Anderson. I also had some important news to report. "Mike, remember I told you last night that the winner of my match has to face Bobby Jackson?"

"Sure."

"Well, check this out: Jackson was upset today."

"Wow, the third seed out in the second round! Who'd he lose to?"

"Some guy from Chicago named Eddie Binder. I've never even heard of him."

"Even still, Bryan, don't get too comfortable. This guy Binder just beat the third seed. He's gonna have some serious momentum."

"You're right, Mike." I smiled, knowing that I had lucked out by having Mike as my new coach. Henry had made sure another coach was in place to help me carry on. "Oh hey, Mike, guess what? I saw a photo of you on the Wall of Champions, you're a Kalamazoo legend!"

Mike chuckled, "I don't know if I would go *that* far. I did win the tournament many years ago, so I'm happy to hear that I'm still remembered."

"Yeah, but what was up with your hair back then?" I kidded.

"Don't remind me," Mike laughed. "And speaking of bad hair, I have a message for you. I played in a doubles match today at The Courts with your good buddy, Jimmy Ellis. He told me to wish you luck. As usual, he was playing some great tennis, and acting like a clown in between sets!"

I laughed, "Good ol' Jimmy. He'll never change."

The next day, I faced unseeded Eddie Binder. He was a player who had a very unusual game. He didn't seem to hit the ball too solidly. Warming up, I thought, *This guy is not that good.* But he had obviously been good enough to beat the third seed.

Even after we had played an hour of tennis, it seemed like Binder hadn't hit one clean shot. I couldn't believe he was up a set *and* a break of serve! My strategy of pounding every ball wasn't working. As a matter of fact, it seemed to be playing right into the hands of my clever opponent.

Henry had always told me to change a game plan if it wasn't working. So I started easing up on my groundstrokes. I went to heavy topspin on my shots. This slight change had a real effect on Binder. No longer able to rely on my power, he was forced to create his own. That wasn't nearly as comfortable for him. The momentum started to shift and the match slowly began to turn. By the time it was 3-all in the third, we were both very tired. The match had become a test of courage as well as skill. I felt like I was ready to collapse.

But I had been in situations like this many times before—especially during practice, when Henry simply wouldn't let me quit. I smiled, because I could just see the old man yelling at me and telling one of his tennis stories. Thinking about Henry at that moment made me feel good. It also gave me some much-needed energy.

Ignoring how tired I felt, I stepped up to meet this difficult test. I was determined to stay out there and win the match. Binder obviously felt the same way, and he continued to fight. Finally, twenty-five minutes later, he started to weaken. I pulled ahead and won it, 7-5 in the third set.

That night I was exhausted, but I also felt a rush of excitement. I was still in the tournament! I had the next day off, which would give me some rest. Then I would play my round of sixteen match on Wednesday. My opponent was the number thirteen seed, Jason Turner, of Copper Mountain, Colorado.

I tried to keep my mind off the next match. I just wanted to appreciate what I had already accomplished. Nothing could change the fact that I had reached the round of sixteen—the fourth round—at the National Championships. Many famous tennis champions had competed at Kalamazoo. It was thrilling to realize that I was now also a small part of the history of this legendary tournament.

After breakfast the next morning I took the hotel shuttle bus over to Kalamazoo College. This was where the tournament was being held. My parents were taking Brandon to get a haircut and then do a little sightseeing. We made plans to meet up again around noon for lunch. Then I would practice later in the afternoon to prepare for my next match.

When I got to Kalamazoo College, I went looking for Henry's old friend, Charlie Morrison. As Henry had predicted, it wasn't very hard to find him. Everybody knew Charlie. He was a popular sportswriter who had covered the Nationals for more than forty years. He was retired, but he still came out every year to enjoy the tennis. I found him relaxing at an outdoor table. He was sipping iced tea from a tall glass as he read the newspaper.

"Excuse me, Mr. Morrison?" I approached his table with a smile.

"Yes?" The old sportswriter put down the newspaper and looked up.

"My name is Bryan Berry. An old friend of yours, Henry Johnson, asked me to look you up. He wanted me to say hello for him."

Morrison's face lit up like a lightbulb, "Henry Johnson! I haven't spoken to him in years. Please, sit down."

"Thanks," I said. Putting my tennis bag on the ground, I sat down across from Morrison.

"Now, how do you know Henry?"

"He was my coach for the last couple of years. He just passed away about two months ago." It was still an incredibly painful thing to say.

"Oh my, I'm so sorry to hear that. They never made them any finer than Henry, that's for sure. We were friends back in California, nearly fifty years ago. Henry was one of the best-known coaches on the West Coast. But I thought he stopped doing that years and years ago. Did you say he was *your* coach?"

"Yes, sir, he sure was. I'm aware that he hadn't done it in a long time. But all I know is that he made me into a tennis player. I wouldn't be sitting here right now if it weren't for him."

"That sounds like the Henry I knew. Understood the game better than anyone I've ever seen, and I've seen 'em all. Nobody could get more out of a player than he could." Morrison smiled. "Back in our day, everybody wanted Henry as a coach for their kid. Parents of tennis stars would offer him money and all kinds of things. A Hollywood producer even offered to put Henry in the movies!"

I tried to picture it and started laughing. "Henry could have been a movie star! That's kinda funny."

"Henry could have been anything, son. But he gave it all up." Morrison shrugged his shoulders. "It's a real shame, too. I've always felt sad that certain things happened the way they did. Otherwise, I believe he could have been a real coaching legend." Morrison's face was calm, but his voice was very emotional.

"You mean…if Johnny hadn't died?"

Morrison looked at me for a long moment. "Yes, that changed everything for Henry. Did he tell you a lot about Johnny?" I nodded. "I'm not surprised," Morrison said. "Johnny Matthews had the prettiest game I ever saw in my life. There's no doubt in my mind that he would have been one of the great ones. What a tragedy." Morrison sighed. "And what a blow to Henry," he added.

"They were real close, huh?"

"Yes," Morrison said. "I'm sure you gathered that by the way Henry talked about him, right?"

"Yeah, it was like he was talking about his own kid."

Morrison took a sip of his iced tea and changed

the subject. "Now, son, tell me about yourself. Any student of Henry's must be good. He always knew talent when he saw it."

I ended up telling Morrison the whole story. I began with the first Courage Open, when Henry approached me after the loss to Ted Grover. Morrison listened closely as I described everything that happened. For him, hearing this story about Henry Johnson was like being back together with a long-lost friend. It was difficult for me to talk about Henry getting sick and then suffering the heart attack. Even Morrison's eyes were moist. But he wanted to hear about everything, including Henry's illness. He was thrilled that Henry inspired me to shine in the Missouri Valley Supers Circuit.

"Son, I'm happy he lived long enough to hear you were going to the nationals. I *know* how much that meant to him. You gave him a wonderful gift."

I was speechless for a moment. It never occurred to me that I might have given Henry so much. All I knew for certain was that he had given me everything. "I sure appreciate hearing you say that, Mr. Morrison. I figured nothing could make up for Johnny never getting the chance to be a star."

"I would have agreed with you, Bryan, but not after what I've just heard. There's no doubt in my mind that you were as dear to Henry as Johnny was. And that puts you in good company."

"Thank you, sir."

Both of us stood up, and Morrison looked at

me thoughtfully as we shook hands. "Good luck in your match tomorrow, son. Whether you win or lose, let me tell you something—wherever he is right now, I bet Henry is real proud of you."

CHAPTER TWELVE

THE KID FROM COURAGE

Henry had spoken about a moment when everything would come together for me. He had compared it to a surfer riding a wave. After winning two more matches, it was more like a tidal wave.

Incredibly, I had become the talk of the National Championships. Newspaper articles printed stories with headlines like: "Unknown Takes Nationals by Storm" and "The Kid from Courage Wins Again." There were interviews, even an appearance on a local television show!

In the round of sixteen, I beat Jason Turner, the thirteenth seed. A left-handed player, he had amazing talent but very little mental toughness. He reminded me of Jimmy Ellis. Although Turner hit some unbelievable shots, he also missed a lot of easy ones. I had figured out my game plan quickly: keep the ball in the court and fight for every point. Our different styles made for some very entertaining tennis. I was a smart, aggressive baseliner, while Turner was a flashy player. In the end, I was just a little too solid for him, winning, 6-4, 7-5.

That victory put me into the quarters, where I won again. I beat the number six seed, Seth Green, 6-3 in the third. A great serve-and-volleyer, Green found himself with a big problem. He was matched up against an opponent who was returning serve very confidently. Green started going for too much on his serve, which caused him to start missing. The sixteen-year-old from Arizona fought hard, but I was on a roll. I was simply playing perfect tennis.

It was now Friday, a day off for me. The semis were the next day. My plans were to relax, and then practice in the afternoon. I definitely needed some rest—my body was feeling very tired from all the tennis I'd been playing. Brandon and I hung out at Kalamazoo College, where I had become pretty well known. People were actually coming up to talk to me or wish me luck. A few even asked for autographs! It was quite an experience for two small-town kids. We certainly weren't used to this kind of attention.

The next day, I faced the number two seed, Shawn Robertson. A sixteen-year-old from Atlanta, Robertson was an explosive baseliner. He was an outstanding athlete who was very tough mentally—all the qualities of a fantastic tennis player.

As the match began, I was calm. I told myself that a defeat wouldn't take away from my accomplishments. In fact, it was Robertson who was nervous. Although he was the number two player in the entire nation, he was a little banged-up physically. He had injured his left ankle earlier in the week, and it was still very sore. Making matters worse, he was aware that he was facing an opponent who had nothing to lose.

Robertson was clearly playing at less than one hundred percent because of his injury. Still, he was a talented and dangerous tennis player. We were thrilling the crowd with long and exciting rallies. As the first set went into a tiebreaker, the match was completely up for grabs.

Being the underdog, I had the support of the crowd. That didn't bother Robertson at all. He was having enough trouble on the court without worrying about anything else. He tried to forget about his injured ankle, but I could tell it was bothering him. Still, this was going to be a competitive tiebreaker that could make or break the match for me. Before I served the first point, Henry's familiar words entered my mind: *The game that gets you there won't win it for you.*

Over the course of the tiebreaker, both of us raised our games to produce some tremendous tennis. With Henry's words dancing in my head, I was hitting the ball as hard as I could. Robertson wasn't letting up either. He had obviously decided that his sore ankle wouldn't be able to take too much more.

He *had* to win this set.

By the time it was 11-all in the tiebreaker, both of us had saved three set points. The crowd was going wild. Robertson belted a blazing first serve, which forced me to hit a short return. He charged to the net behind a big topspin forehand. I got there and totally fooled him with a looping crosscourt backhand. To the delight of the crowd, I now had another set point—this time on my own serve. I hit a high-kicking serve to Robertson's backhand and rushed to the net. Robertson tried to chip his return low, but the ball floated softly through the air. I jumped on it and easily put the volley away. I had just won the first set by winning the tiebreaker, 13-11.

Robertson was discouraged. Had he pulled out the first set, his experience might have helped him squeak out a victory. Now, especially with a bad ankle, he was in trouble. He fought bravely for a little while longer, but I overpowered him, 7-6, 6-3. The Kid from Courage was in the finals of the National Championships!

From the moment I walked off the court, it was insane. It seemed like everyone wanted a piece of me. They wanted pictures and interviews. Some college coaches handed me their business cards. I was grateful that my family was with me. They swept me out of there and we went straight back to the hotel. Mom answered all of the phone calls that were coming in. Meanwhile, I tried to relax and keep my mind off the finals.

The next day, I tried to appear calm as I warmed up. However, it was overwhelming to hear the umpire's voice echo throughout Stowe Stadium: "And to my right, a player who has beaten three seeds to reach the finals. From Courage, Kansas: Bryan Berry!" The crowd responded with a thunderous standing ovation. It sent chills up and down my spine. I felt a surge of nervous energy as I took a quick look around the enormous stadium. What an awesome sight! Thousands of tennis fans had gathered here on this beautiful summer afternoon for one reason: to see if I could pull off one of the greatest upsets in the history of junior tennis.

My opponent today was Danny Gold, the best sixteen-year-old in the United States. He was said to be one of the most promising American juniors in the last ten years. Watching his face as we were warming up, I could tell that he was feeling very confident.

"Ladies and gentlemen, this match will be two out of three sets. Mr. Gold has won the toss and he has elected to serve first. Players ready?" The umpire looked around for a second. "Play!"

The first point of the match showed some very impressive tennis. Both of us were crushing the ball during a long baseline rally. Finally, a short ball gave me the opening I wanted. I moved forward, pounding my approach shot crosscourt as I charged to the net. Gold raced to the corner and hit the ball on the dead run. He passed me with a spectacular forehand up the line. The crowd burst into applause as I glanced at my opponent. *Oh, man, you really are as good as everybody says!*

Danny Gold easily held serve and we switched sides. I was determined to serve big and show Gold that I could hang with him. I opened up by blasting my first serve, a bullet that found the line. 15-love. I went for it again, but Gold was ready this time. Catching the ball early, he attacked the net behind a good return that forced me out of position. He completed the point by punching a shoulder-high volley into the open court.

Three points later Gold had the first break chance of the match. My first serve caught the net and fell back. Gold crept inside the baseline, looking to hit and come to the net. His approach shot stayed low and I tried to answer with a topspin lob. But it wasn't nearly deep enough. Gold easily put it away, and—just like that—it was 2-love.

After Gold held serve again, I started to feel a little discouraged. It was early, but this was the exact beginning I had feared. Usually, I wouldn't be too worried about finding myself down a quick break of serve. But this was not a normal match. Not with the brilliant Danny Gold on the other side of the net. I ordered myself to stay mentally tough and battle for every point.

There was no doubt about who was in charge. Danny Gold won the first set easily, 6-2. The top seed was in the driver's seat. A gifted athlete, he had also won at Kalamazoo the previous year. He seemed determined that nothing would prevent him from winning back-to-back crowns.

As the second set began, we stayed on serve through the first three games. Then, all of a sudden, Gold started returning serve more aggressively. I tried to hold him off, but he was just too skilled. Finally, on break point, he hit a beautiful drop volley to win the game. After holding serve, he was in control with a commanding 4-1 lead.

I tried to gather my thoughts as I sat down and took a long drink of water. I realized that the match was slipping away from me. It certainly wasn't a disgrace to lose to the best player in the nation. Gold had been heavily favored coming into the match. A quick glance up at the scoreboard told the story loud and clear:

	1	2	3
D. Gold	6	4	
B. Berry	2	1	

I considered changing strategy. But to what? *If I hit and come in, I get passed. It's impossible to out-steady this guy. And I sure don't want to give him a chance to attack the net.* What would Henry tell me if he were here? My mind wandered back to those many long days of practice. The old man had taught me that no problem was too great to overcome. He had taught me to believe in myself.

I also thought about Johnny Matthews. I recalled Henry's words about how Johnny loved everything about tennis. I knew that Johnny would have been thrilled just to be here right now. Win or lose, he would have welcomed the challenge. With Henry in the stands cheering him on, Johnny would have kept battling. In honor of both Henry and Johnny, I couldn't quit now.

I began to fight—harder than I had ever fought before. Blocking everything else out of my mind, I played like every point was match point. I started making a comeback. I got the break of serve back somehow. Then, I used every last ounce of energy in my body to get the second set into a tiebreaker. Putting everything on the line, I pulled out the tiebreaker, 8-6. Amazingly, it was one set all.

The crowd was going crazy. They had really grown to like me. Most of the credit for that had to go to my new friend, Charlie Morrison. He had come out of retirement to write an article about me. They put it on the front page of the *Kalamazoo Gazette!* Morrison told the entire story. He described how I had gone from an ordinary tennis player to a contender at Kalamazoo. He also talked about Johnny. He explained how two kids, more than fifty years apart, were linked together by one thing—a coach who helped them realize their dreams. I was grateful to Mr. Morrison for letting the world know about Henry. I was proud that the old man finally got the credit he deserved.

I had used up all my energy winning the second set. Making it even tougher, this was my seventh match in nine days. By the time it was 1-all in the third, I was completely worn out. After being shocked by my comeback, Gold took charge once again. He broke my serve and then held for a 3-1 lead.

As the match started to draw to an end, the crowd continued to support me. They appreciated the fact that I wasn't giving up. Even though defeat was now almost certain, I was still trying as hard as I could. With Gold serving at 5-2, I refused to pack it in. Going for it all, I sent the game to seven thrilling deuces. I saved five match points along the way.

When Gold finally won the match by hitting a booming overhead on his sixth match point, the crowd cheered loudly. I was so tired that I could barely stand up. Still, I forced myself to make my way forward to congratulate the champion. Gold didn't shake my hand. Instead, he jumped over the net—without saying one word, he put his arm around my shoulder. We walked over to the sidelines together and took a bow.

Everyone in the stadium felt that they had witnessed something incredible. Ten days earlier, I had been a total unknown. Now, as the tournament was coming to an end, everyone knew the name Bryan Berry. I had given the great Danny Gold an exciting challenge. I was certain we would face off again in the future.

I waited as they set everything up for the awards ceremony. Exhausted, I sat quietly in my chair at courtside. Some photographers were taking pictures of me for tennis magazines, but I wasn't paying any attention to them. I had a lot of things on my mind. It was satisfying to realize that my tennis had unlimited potential, pointing to a bright future. It was all because of my coach—and my friend—Henry Johnson. *Henry, look what we did together, you and I. We went the distance, and this is only the beginning.*

I looked up from the towel and searched the stands for my family. I smiled when I saw them. My mom was laughing and crying at the same time, wiping away tears. I waved to her. Brandon was jumping up and down and giving me the thumbs-up sign. Dad was juggling a camcorder in one hand and a camera in the other. I felt good knowing they were there with me. Only one thing would have made it complete: I wished Henry had been there too.

I missed my coach dearly, and I knew that nothing would ever be the same without him. But I also knew that the spirit of our friendship was like an unbreakable bond. It would always remain a part of me.

I wondered what Henry would say if he were standing there with me at that moment. I laughed out loud. Probably something like, "Good work, kid. Now let's get done with this ceremony and get back home. We've got a lot of work to do."

TEST YOURSELF...ARE YOU A PRO-FESSIONAL READER?

Chapter 1: A Funny Old Man

Who wins the practice match between Bryan and Jimmy? What is the final score? Describe the final point of the match.

Twelve years earlier, the town of Courage, Kansas, built a club called "The Courage Courts and Recreation Club." However, nobody calls it by its full name. What does everybody call it? Describe the club (how many tennis courts, etc.).

Who is Henry Johnson? Tell one or two of his interesting tennis stories.

ESSAY

Nothing in the world is more important to Bryan than tennis. Talk about a sport, or an activity (music, art, reading, etc.) that you are enthusiastic about. Explain how you became interested in it, and why it is important to you.

Chapter 2: The Courage Open

When Jimmy says that the score of his match was "two bagels," what does he mean?

Who is Mike Scully? List one or more of his accomplishments.

What is Bryan's "big weapon" in tennis, as he describes it? By comparison, which of his strokes are not nearly as good?

ESSAY

As he checks out the draw, Jimmy Ellis shows a lot of confidence that he will easily reach the quarterfinals of the Courage Open tournament. Do you consider yourself to be a confident person? When you are faced with a difficult situation—like an important test, or sports competition—do you look forward to the challenge or do you get nervous at the very thought of it? Explain your answer.

Chapter 3: Afraid to Lose

Ted Grover lives up to his reputation as a "lowdown cheater" by doing something at the end of the second set against Bryan. Detail Grover's actions, and also describe what Grover looks like.

What happens when Bryan is sitting by himself after his discouraging loss to Ted Grover?

What does Henry Johnson look like, and what is Bryan's guess as to how old he is?

ESSAY

Some of the adults at The Courts see Henry Johnson as a crazy old man who has "lost it." Yet Bryan is amazed that Mr. Johnson has so much good sense and understanding. Who is the older person in your life (parent, grandparent, teacher, etc.) that you can talk to about anything? What kinds of things have you learned from this person? Describe the relationship you have with him/her.

Chapter 4: Coach

In response to Mr. Johnson's question, what does Bryan say his goal is in tennis over the next couple of years?

After losing a practice match to Jimmy, Bryan mentions that he has been practicing with Mr. Johnson. What is Jimmy's reaction?

When Bryan gets home after his first practice with his new coach, he is exhausted. Why? From that point on, how often do he and Mr. Johnson train?

ESSAY

Mr. Johnson uses the expression "no pain, no gain," to teach Bryan that we all have to work hard in order to accomplish things—even if it takes a lot of time. Describe something you have done—a project for school, reading a long book, working hard to become a better player—that took a long time. Did you feel good after you accomplished it? Was it worth all the time and effort you put into it?

Chapter 5: Johnny Matthews

When Johnny Matthews was thirteen years old, he started hanging around the Los Angeles Tennis Club. What did he do there? What was he doing when Mr. Johnson caught him in the members lounge after hours?

During dinner, Mr. Johnson entertains Mrs. Johnson and Bryan with stories of his youth. What does he talk about?

Mr. Johnson had once said that Bryan reminds him of Johnny. According to Mr. Johnson, how is Bryan similar to Johnny when it comes to tennis?

ESSAY

Bryan is amazed when he sees all the trophies at Mr. Johnson's house. Have you ever won a trophy, an award, or earned a perfect report card? How did it make you feel? What did you do to earn this honor?

Chapter 6: Summer Vacation

Although Bryan is happy about summer vacation, one bad thing happened. What was it? Why was it a major disappointment?

Why do Bryan and Henry drive for an hour and a half to the city of Wichita, Kansas?

Describe some of the things that Bryan and his family did during their trip to Los Angeles.

ESSAY

Bryan's exciting summer is capped off by a great trip to Los Angeles. Describe the best trip that you have ever taken in your life. Where did you go? Who were you with? What did you do? What was the highlight of the trip?

Chapter 7: The Return of the Courage Open

As he and Bryan warm up for their match, Ted Grover realizes that Bryan is not the same kid he beat one year earlier. What are the differences with Bryan, both physically and with his tennis game?

After defeating Ted Grover, Bryan gives Henry a gift. What is the gift? In the gift, he explains why he is giving it to Henry on this particular day—what is the reason?

What is written on the note that Bryan reads during his match with Mike Scully? What is the message that Henry is trying to send to Bryan?

ESSAY

Bryan turns in a fantastic performance at the Courage Open by forcing Mike Scully to a tiebreaker in the second set. Have you ever had the chance to do something special in front of your family or friends (act in a play, give a speech, compete in an athletic event, etc.)? How did this situation make you feel? And if you haven't yet experienced it, is this something that you are willing to work hard for? Explain why it will be worth it to you.

Chapter 8: Preparing for Battle

To reach the nationals, Bryan has to battle the best kids from his "section." Name the five states in his section.

Although Bryan feels ready for the Missouri Valley Supers Circuit, what is the only thing he's bummed out about? Who will be helping him train for the upcoming tournaments?

What is the most difficult situation Bryan faces in his match against Craig Schroeder?

ESSAY

Even though he has already won several tennis matches by now, Bryan has a lousy performance and loses to Eric Davis, the number four seed, 6-1, 6-2. This defeat makes him very anxious, but luckily Henry calms him down. When you have a bad day, or get angry or anxious, how do you deal with it? Who can you talk to about how you feel, and does he/she usually calm you down and make you feel better?

Chapter 9: The Final Piece of the Puzzle

Why is Bryan nervous when he arrives at the Wichita Tennis Club?

What sad event takes place on the very same day that Bryan is scoring his huge win over Ricky Segal? Where does Bryan go as soon as he receives the news?

List the six players that are moving on to the nationals. Upon finding out, what little joke does Henry make about Ted Grover?

ESSAY

Bryan is worried because he knows that Henry is old and obviously very sick. Have you ever visited a member of your family at the hospital and worried about what might happen? How did this situation make you feel? Explain.

Chapter 10: From Courage to Kalamazoo

Henry explains that there will be a time when it all comes together for Bryan. He uses an example that involves a surfer. What is the example he uses to make his point?

At the exact moment that Bryan is getting ready to leave the hospital room, what does he realize? What does he then do?

Name the state where the "National Championships" are taking place, and at what point in the summer Bryan and his family hit the road to go there.

ESSAY

Henry had once told Bryan: "It's a long way from Courage from Kalamazoo." Now, Bryan has accomplished his goal. Talk about something you've accomplished in your life, no matter how big or small. What did you do and how did this accomplishment make you feel? Explain.

Chapter 11: Kalamazoo

While on the phone with Mike Scully, Bryan mentions that he saw something on the Wall of Champions. What did he see, and what is Mike's reaction?

What funny story does Charlie Morrison tell Bryan about an offer made to Henry by a Hollywood movie producer?

According to Charlie Morrison, what "wonderful gift" did Bryan give Henry?

ESSAY

Even though he's very tired, Bryan doesn't give up and goes the distance to win his match with Eddie Binder. Describe a time in your life when you had to work extra hard to achieve something (working late at night to finish a school project, winning a game in overtime, etc.). Explain what you did and what gave you the motivation to put forth the extra effort.

Chapter 12: The Kid from Courage

Where do Bryan and Brandon hang out on Bryan's day off, and what cool things happen there?

The crowd has really grown to like Bryan, and for that he gives most of the credit to Charlie Morrison. What had Morrison come out of retirement to do?

While waiting for the awards ceremony to begin, Bryan has a lot of things on his mind. What is he thinking about?

<u>ESSAY</u>

Memories of Henry and Johnny inspire Bryan to keep fighting and make a comeback against Danny Gold. Who is your hero, and who inspires you?